The
Stolen
Dummy

THE CASE OF THE

STOLEN DUMMY

A BRAINS BENTON MYSTERY

BY GEORGE WYATT

Based on the characters
created by Charles Spain Verral

ILLUSTRATED BY WALTER DEY

A WHITMAN BOOK
Western Publishing Company, Inc., Racine, Wisconsin
WHITMAN is a registered trademark of Western Publishing Company, Inc.

TABLE OF CONTENTS

1 DESPERATE CHASE

I WAS GASPING FOR BREATH. I WAS SO TIRED MY LEGS WERE MOVING only from memory. All I wanted was to lie down and rest. Yet, I forced myself to stagger on. I couldn't stop. Not now. Not with my pursuer hot on my trail.

And he was still after me. Even though I couldn't see him I was certain that he was somewhere behind me, following like the human bloodhound he was.

I guess most people don't know what it's like to be a hunted criminal and I hope they never will. It's awful, believe me. I found that out that morning in September when I made my wild dash for freedom.

The country I was crossing was wild and rugged. In some places there were great swampy areas and I had to scramble from hummock to hummock to get through. I'd slipped and fallen any number of times. My dungarees were torn, my knees skinned. I was soaking wet from sprawling head first into a pool of water. My hair was caked with mud. And my sneakers felt as if they each weighed a ton.

I must have been running and dodging for almost an hour when suddenly I saw a road ahead. But more important was the sight of a drainpipe that had been built under the road to stop washouts. The drainpipe was a big one—big enough for me to hide in.

I made for it and crawled inside. It was cool and dark in there and quiet. I lay still, listening. All I could hear was the faint sighing of the wind.

After five minutes had passed, I began to think that maybe I'd given my pursuer the slip. *Creeps!* I should have had my head examined. For right then a familiar voice sounded from outside.

"Attention, Two-Gun Carson. I am well aware that you have taken refuge in that culvert. You will kindly emerge with your hands elevated or I shall be forced to take drastic measures to bring about your evacuation."

I didn't answer, hoping against hope that he'd move on.

No such luck. The voice sounded again.

"Silence will avail you nothing but hardship, Two-Gun. If you have not put in an appearance within the space of sixty seconds, I shall have no recourse but to consume the emergency food rations—namely, the apple pie. You read me, Two-Gun?"

"Yeah," I called. "I read you loud and clear. I'm coming."

So I crawled out. There was no sense trying to bluff. He had me cold. I knew when I was licked. Anyway, I was hungry.

I might as well own up right here and now that I've been kind of fooling you about what happened that morning. I mean, my name wasn't Two-Gun Carson. It was Jimmy Carson. And I wasn't an escaped criminal. I was just a kid who lived at 43 Maple Street in the town of Crestwood. As for the person who was pursuing me, why he wasn't my enemy at all. He was, in fact, my best friend and partner, Barclay Benton, better known as "Brains" Benton.

All this carrying on probably sounds as though I've flipped my lid. But I can explain everything.

You see, Brains and I were in business together. We were private investigators. We had our own company, the Benton and Carson International Detective Agency. This was no pretend or make-believe thing. It was for real.

Of course, just because we happened to be a couple of school kids, a lot of people in town didn't take us seriously. For instance, the editor of the *Crestwood Daily Ledger* called us "junior sleuths" and "boy detectives" and sort of patted us on the head. This made us wild because there was nothing little league or juvenile about the cases we took on. *Creeps!* The mysteries we tied into were strictly man-sized, and then some.

But of all the things that got our goat, I think Chief Hadley was the most.

Chief Hadley was the head of the Crestwood Police Department and he never let anyone forget it. He was a big guy with a fancy set of double chins and a stomach the size of a weather balloon and he wore enough gold braid on his uniform and gold stars on his police hat to outfit the Pentagon. He was the law in Crestwood and he couldn't stand for anyone else to get into the act—especially a couple of kids named Brains Benton and Jimmy Carson.

I remember how huffy he got the time Brains tried to tell him his theory of how a jail break had happened—a theory which later proved to be correct.

"Now run along, sonny," the Chief had said, "and play your game of cops and robbers someplace else. And leave criminal matters to us experts."

Chief Hadley was hard to take, all right. But what made it worse was that Brains and I never seemed to get a chance to prove to the old windbag what smart detective work we could really do. And it began to look as if we never would, for there hadn't been a crime or the smell of a crime in Crestwood for weeks and weeks.

Not that Brains was bothered.

"The opportunity to convince Chief Hadley of our worth will present itself in good time, Jimmy," he said to me. "Until it does we must keep ourselves primed for action. That means practicing the skills of our profession, finger-printing, shadowing and the like. A wise man never allows the tools of his trade to grow rusty."

It was because of this that we were out in the country on that particular morning. Brains had decided that we needed to brush up on the art of tracking.

"You'll take the part of an escaped felon fleeing for his life," he'd told me. "I'll give you five minutes' start, then come after you. You must do everything in your power to throw me off your trail."

"O.K.," I'd said. "But you're going to have a hard job running me down."

"Oh, I don't believe so," Brains had said in that irritating way he had. "But we shall see."

So, right after breakfast, we'd left town on our bikes and ridden up into the stretch of wasteland to the southwest of Lake Carmine. There, Brains and I had parted and I'd become not only a desperate criminal on the lam but somebody who was going to show wise guy Brains a thing or two.

Of course, neither of us had had any idea then of the horrible discovery we were to make later that morning or of the load of trouble that was at that very moment racing our way.

Creeps! I'll say we didn't!

2 DREAD DISCOVERY

NOW LET ME GET BACK TO WHERE I WAS CRAWLING OUT OF THAT drainpipe. I'll admit I was madder than a hornet because I hadn't outfoxed Brains and given him the slip. And I got even madder when I came into the bright sunshine and saw my partner. He was leaning lazily back against the trunk of a tree, sort of whistling to himself.

Brains was the once-seen-never-forgotten type. He was extra tall for his age and extra skinny and his hair was more than just extra red. It was the next thing to being on fire. He wore thick-rimmed glasses which gave him a solemn, owlish look. He liked to think that he resembled the famous detective, Sherlock Holmes. And in some ways he did, mostly because of a large bony nose.

But what struck me now about him wasn't any of this. It was simply how clean he looked. Here he'd been through the same berry patches and across the same swampy places that I had. But there wasn't a spot on his shirt. His pants still held a press. And his shoes were dry and mudless.

13

As for me, I gave all the appearance of having been in a rooting contest with a bunch of pigs. Brains noticed my condition right away. And he grinned as if he'd seen something funny.

"You seem to be in excellent shape—for a laundromat, Jimmy," he said. "If your mother could only see you now."

"So what!" I said. "I had an accident. I fell into a pool of water."

Brains nodded. "Quite so. I watched you."

That jolted me. I'd thought at the time I'd been far ahead of him.

"You watched me?" I said.

"Yes, indeed. I was approximately a hundred yards behind you when it happened," Brains said. "But don't be concerned, Jimmy. You enacted the role of a fugitive from justice remarkably well. You even made the obvious blunders that a person with such a limited mentality would make."

I came to a quick boil.

"You were shot with luck to be able to follow me!" I snapped.

Brains looked down his long nose at me.

"Luck entered into this tracking exercise not in the slightest degree," he said deliberately. "You left a clearly defined trail which was simplicity itself to follow at all times. For instance, shortly after you departed from me you crossed the road by climbing a pine tree, working your way out on a limb and dropping to the ground on the other side. I found a little pine bough in the road, freshly broken off."

"Well, O.K.," I muttered.

"You then recrossed the road, walking backward. Your heels sank deeper than they should. I'll admit you concealed your footprints in the woods quite deftly until you came to that patch of raspberries."

My eyes bugged out. "How in the Sam Hill did you . . . ?"

"Knee prints. You crushed some of the berries. I never knew

you to pass up raspberries. It was right after that that you fell into the water."

Brains took off his glasses. He polished them carefully before going on. "You lost your temper and got careless. You left tracks all the way to that deserted farm. You snagged your jeans on the barbed wire fence. I found threads caught in one of the barbs. Of course, your tracks were quite obvious going down through the farmyard. When dew is still on the grass you can see where people walk. Even if you hadn't left tracks, I would have been aware that you had gone that way."

I squinted up at him. "How?"

"Did you notice that tumble-down corncrib?" Brains asked. I said I had.

"A flock of crows had been at some corn that was left in it. When crows are eating, they always leave a lookout. About a dozen crows took off as soon as the lookout saw you and started cawing his throat out. You must have heard him, Jimmy."

I kept quiet. I had nothing to say.

"As for your finally taking refuge in this culvert," Brains paused and gestured to some tall weeds that grew by the entrance to the drainpipe, "you will note that the heads of a number of those weeds have been broken very recently, clearly from the passage of some large object—presumably a human. And since we apparently are the only humans out this way right now . . ."

Brains shrugged and stopped talking. He didn't have to go on. He'd handed me the whole business, chapter and verse. He'd known practically every step I'd taken, if not every breath.

You can see from this that my partner hadn't been nicknamed Brains for nothing. He was so doggone smart it hurt. I think it was this very smartness that sometimes got under my skin and made me mad. Here I was, just an ordinary everyday kid with a face full of freckles who brought home a so-so report card teamed up with a genius. Talk about stress and strain.

Of course, Brains came by his gray matter naturally enough. After all, his parents weren't exactly morons. His father was a professor of ancient history at Crestwood College. And his mother was on the staff of the college, too. She was a painter and a good one. She taught in the art department.

Don't go getting the idea from what I've told you that Brains was any part of a sissy or an odd ball. Far from it. He was easily the best pitcher our school ever had. I'll admit winning games didn't matter to him, but the various scientific methods of whipping the ball through the strike zone did. Brains was one of the most popular kids at school. Especially around exam time. That guy had a sure-fire method of drilling you in math so that the stuff stuck—for long enough anyway.

Now as I looked at him, lolled back against that tree trunk, I remembered something of vital importance.

"All right," I said. "You tracked me. And you trapped me. You made me come out of my hiding place. But where is that food you threatened to eat?"

Brains laughed.

"Trust you to think of that, Jimmy," he said.

He had a knapsack on his back and he now slung it around and unfastened the strap. From inside, Brains removed a cardboard container in which was a delicious-looking pie. The pie had already been cut in half and Brains handed me one portion.

"Compliments of Mrs. Ray," he said. "I only hope the poor creature doesn't expend too much energy searching for her work of art before she finds my note stating that I have borrowed it. Of course, it may take her a little time to translate the Latin."

Mrs. Ray was the Bentons' housekeeper. She was a fussy little woman who didn't approve of Brains or how his parents were allowing him to grow up. And she didn't hesitate to say so. She and Brains had been conducting a running feud for a long time. Brains making off with the pie after the housekeeper had gone to great pains to hide it from him was just one more round.

But for all of Mrs. Ray's faults, I had to admit that she sure could bake pies. This one tasted terrific.

It's funny how things happen. I mean, if we hadn't taken time to eat that pie, we might have gone by way of the road back to where we'd left our bikes, instead of striking across country. And if we'd done that, we wouldn't have passed Boiling Pond and seen the "thing" that lay at the bottom of those clear cold waters.

We had polished off the last crumbs of the pie when Brains realized how late it was getting to be.

"We'd better head for town, Jimmy," he said. "It's eleven-thirty. Didn't your mother tell you to be sure to be home in time for lunch?"

"Yeah," I said. "But we can make it."

"Only if we leave at once and follow a direct overland route to our bicycles," he said. He took a compass from his pocket and studied it. "Our machines are directly south by southwest from where we are now standing. Come along."

Brains immediately set off at such a brisk pace that I had to break into a trot to keep up.

"I hope you'll be able to slip up to your room and change your clothes before your mother sees you," Brains said. "She won't be too enthusiastic about your soiled condition."

This sort of thing was typical of Brains. I mean, he was always going out of his way not to rile either of our families, even in little things. Of course, I knew why. So far, both sets of parents had been very lenient about our detective work. They'd let us have a lot of freedom.

But Brains knew and so did I that if his father and mother or mine ever got upset about something we'd done, the rug could easily be pulled out from under us. And the result might mean curtains for the Benton and Carson International Detective Agency.

However, I wasn't worried about Mom blowing her top over seeing me all messed up. And I told Brains so.

"My mother is in such a good mood over that Community Camp Fund drive," I said, "that I could walk in tarred and feathered and she wouldn't bat an eye."

"I wouldn't count on it, Jimmy," Brains said. "Women, and mothers in particular, have a most disconcerting way of undergoing sudden changes."

Even so, I still wasn't worried, no matter what he said. After all, Brains hadn't seen that look of satisfaction on my mother's face when she'd got home last night.

You see, my mother was a joiner. She was a member of the Garden Club, the Civic Improvement Club, the Women Voters League and a dozen others. And when somebody in town came up with the idea that Crestwood should have a community camp where the local kids could go, my mother was one of the first to start beating the drums. In less than no time a flock of the women in town, and Brains' mother was with them, began a drive to raise money for permanent cabins and stuff. The drive had ended the previous night with the workers turning in the money. Mom, herself, had collected almost four hundred dollars. And the total, in cash and checks, came to five thousand bucks and a few cents. The dough had been handed over to Mr. Harvey Beal, the real estate man. And he had placed it in his office safe until it could be deposited in the bank in the morning.

I'm telling you all this for a very good reason, as you'll find out later.

Well, Brains kept up his fast pace and so did I. The sun had gone behind a pile of clouds but the air was still sticky hot. There was something about this stretch of country that made you feel uneasy. It looked like the landscape you might find on a dead planet . . . real spooky and scary. I can't honestly say that I had a hunch that danger lay ahead for us. But I did feel tensed up and I wanted to get back to town.

I guess we'd been going along for ten or fifteen minutes when Brains suddenly pointed.

"Unless I'm very much mistaken," he said, "Boiling Pond is just over that ridge ahead. You've never seen the Pond, have you, Jimmy?"

"No," I said.

Of course, I'd heard of it. Everybody around Crestwood had. Boiling Pond had been quite a curiosity in its day. Where the pond stood had once been a dry gravel pit. But somebody, around twenty years ago, had dug too deep, and he'd hit a spring. Water had come gushing up to completely fill the whole pit. A constant stream of bubbles still floated up from the spring, giving the pond its name. A small stream formed at one side to take care of the overflow.

A moment after Brains had spoken we came over the ridge, and there, a few yards beyond, was a large body of water. It formed an almost perfect circle.

"Well, I was right," Brains said. "Boiling Pond."

"How did you know where it was?" I asked him. I'd thought he was as much a stranger to this section as I was.

Brains laughed. "I wish I could give you a complicated answer, but I can't. I knew where it was simply because Mr. Parslow showed it to me when we drove up through here last month."

I recalled then the fishing trip Brains had taken with Will Parslow, the town's tinkerer and handyman. They'd gone up to Lake Carmine to try out a revolutionary rod and reel which Brains and Mr. Parslow had jointly invented.

"Come on," he said to me over his shoulder. "I want you to see how amazingly clear this water is. You can count every pebble on the bottom, twenty feet down."

Any further thought about Will Parslow I might have had was wiped from my mind. And I'm quite sure I would have had a hard time believing anybody if he'd told me at that moment just how deeply this quiet little man with the limp would affect my life, and Brains', too.

As I hurried to catch up with Brains, I became suddenly aware of how still and silent everything was. The surface of the pond was almost smooth. Tiny ripples spread out from a spot on the far side where the spring was.

Brains went to the very edge of the pit. He lowered himself to his knees, then stretched out full length, his head over the rim of the pool. I heard him gasp. He turned his face toward me, and it was white as milk.

"Come here, Jimmy," he said. "Do you see anything down there?"

I stretched out alongside Brains, bracing myself with the heels of my hands. I stared down into the water. It was very clear, yet, for a while, I didn't notice anything unusual. Then something began to take shape. Something was on the bottom, about twenty feet below the surface.

"Creeps!" I said. "It . . . it looks like a car."

"It's an automobile, all right," Brains said. "But there's something hanging out the side of the car."

I put my face closer to the water. A cold lump as big as a turkey egg began to form under my breastbone. Projecting from the window of the car were the head and shoulders and one dangling arm of what certainly appeared to be a human figure.

I stumbled to my feet. I tried to speak, but the words caught in my throat. All I wanted to do was run.

Brains' face was still white. He stood up and backed away.

"This is too serious to keep from the police," he said in a small voice.

"You c-can bet your s-s-sweet life it is," I said. "Let's make tracks. Chief Hadley will listen to us *this* time."

We skirted the south end of the pond until we came to an old woods road that had obviously led to the gravel pit in its day. The road was overgrown with grass and choked with weeds.

Brains suddenly stopped and bent down.

"Look here," he said tensely. "Tire marks . . . fresh ones. And look at those weeds, they're all bent over in one direction."

There was no doubt about it. A car had been driven up the old road and its tracks led right to the edge of the pond and disappeared.

Brains was now down on his hands and knees inspecting the tracks.

"Nobody in his right mind would come up a little-used road like this one and accidentally drive into the pond." He spoke quietly, as if talking to himself.

"Then, if it wasn't an accident," I said, "it must have been a . . . a . . ."

Brains nodded. "Yes, Jimmy," he said. "It must have been a murder!"

3 DOUBLE TROUBLE

As soon as we hit Crestwood, we headed for the police station, pedaling like crazy. Old Sergeant Hawkins was at the desk. He held up his hand when Brains yipped that we had to see Chief Hadley right away.

"Hold on, son," Sergeant Hawkins said. "The Chief's mighty busy. You'd better tell me what's got you so het up."

Brains didn't hesitate. He gave out with a quick account of what we'd discovered.

I'll say this for the sergeant: maybe he was suffering from bunions but he sure lost no time legging it across the hall to the Chief's office. But the big surprise came a moment later when who should appear but Chief Hadley himself. He came out of his office like a tidal wave on the loose and with him were two men. One was Harvey Beal, the real estate man, who had taken care of the Community Camp Fund overnight. The other was the *Crestwood Daily Ledger's* top reporter, Lew Jarman.

I was too excited just then to wonder how come they happened to be with Chief Hadley.

"What's this about finding a body?" the Chief rumbled. "I'm in no mood for horseplay, boys."

"We've been out at Boiling Pond," Brains said. "We discovered that there is an automobile at the bottom, approximately twenty feet down."

"And there's a body in it," I cut in. "I saw it! I saw it!"

"Furthermore," Brains said—he seemed very calm now, and deliberate, the way he always got when he was analyzing a crime—"the car and its occupant haven't been in the water long. I would hazard a guess that submersion took place not earlier than last night."

Chief Hadley's eyes bugged out like a couple of marbles. "How do you know that, Benton? This is no time for making up fancy stories."

Brains gave him a long look over the top of his glasses which had slipped down his nose.

"I base my deductions on these facts," he said. "We discovered tire tracks leading right to the pond. These tracks were very clear and had obviously been made sometime *after* that heavy downpour of rain which occurred late yesterday afternoon."

Harvey Beal had been listening intently to every word Brains had said. He was a short, thin man in his middle age and he made no secret that he was very upset about something. He kept pulling nervously at his fingers.

"Ye gods, Chief!" Harvey Beal exclaimed abruptly. "If this thing happened last night, maybe it has some connection with the robbery. Maybe there were two thieves in on the job and one double-crossed the other and got rid of the corpse in the pond."

Robbery! What robbery? I could see that Brains was as startled as I was over this new development.

"Ridiculous, Harvey!" Chief Hadley boomed. "First off, how

can we be sure that these two boys are telling the truth? You know how they like to play detective."

I distinctly heard Brains' angry intake of breath.

It was at that precise moment that Lew Jarman spoke up. The reporter had been standing apart from the group, almost as if he hadn't been interested. But I knew he was. Lew Jarman was a smart apple and a nice guy.

"If I may make a suggestion, Chief," the reporter said mildly, "it might be worth while to go out to Boiling Pond. Just to check on the facts. And it might be handy if Officer McKeon brought his skin-diving equipment along so he could make an underwater inspection if it should be necessary."

Chief Hadley pulled at his double chin. "Exactly what I'd planned to do," he said. "Took the words right out of my mouth, Jarman."

The Chief swung around and started barking orders to Sergeant Hawkins.

"Get hold of McKeon. And hurry it up. Tell him to bring diving gear."

Lew Jarman winked at us. I went over to him. So did Brains.

"What's this robbery about?" Brains asked. He kept his voice lowered.

The reporter turned to Harvey Beal. "Mr. Beal can tell you more than I can," he said.

"Boys," Harvey Beal said, "a dreadful thing has happened. Somebody broke into my office last night. They jimmied the safe and stole all the Community Camp Fund money. There was five thousand dollars there. Most of it was in cash, but there were some checks, too."

Man, that really rocked me. All the money that Mom and Brains' mother and all the other women had worked so hard to get was now gone.

"But who would pull a dirty trick like that?" I said.

"Your guess is as good as mine," Lew Jarman said. He glanced out of the corner of his eye in Brains' direction. "Any theories building up in that head of yours, Brains?"

Lew was one of the few people who really respected Brains for what he was. He never talked down to us or kidded about our detective work . . . and he wasn't now.

"No theories yet," Brains said. He turned and walked slowly across the big hall of the police station. He had his hands clasped behind his back.

I went with him and I heard him say, "Mr. Beal's conjecture that there might be a connection between the robbery and the occurrence at Boiling Pond might well prove valid."

Brains always talked as if he were reading from a dictionary. It wasn't put on at all.

In a surprisingly short space of time Officer McKeon showed up at the station toting his skin-diving equipment. He'd been contacted by radio.

I honestly believe that Chief Hadley hadn't intended taking Brains and me along when the expedition left for Boiling Pond. And he mightn't have done it except for Lew Jarman.

"I'll be interested to hear the boys' account at the actual scene of the crime," the reporter said.

"Yes," the Chief said. "There will be no room for exaggeration there."

So when Chief Hadley's big official car pulled away from the station house, I was riding in the front seat beside the driver. And Brains was in the back between the Chief and Officer McKeon. Lew Jarman's car was right behind us with Harvey Beal accompanying the reporter. I could see the card that said PRESS stuck in the windshield.

I have to admit that I felt pretty important in the Chief's car with the siren blaring. Especially when we went zipping past that stinker, Stony Rhodes. He was standing at the curb in front of Bennett's Drugstore. And you would've thought he was at the doctor's saying, "Ah," the way his mouth dropped open when he saw me. Of course, I pretended that he didn't exist.

I wondered if Brains was feeling as big as I was. I glanced back at him. He had his arms folded and his legs crossed and he was talking to Chief Hadley as if they were the same age.

"To judge from the tracks we examined," Brains was saying, "all the tires on the car are old and well worn. I predict that the submerged car itself may be in the same condition."

I noticed Chief Hadley wince.

"Leave those details to the police department, Benton," he growled.

It didn't seem to take any time before we'd left the macadam and swung into the old road that led to Boiling Pond. It was pretty rough going, and the shock absorbers and springs on the Chief's car got a real workout. The driver braked the car to a stop close to the edge of the pond, and we all got out.

Brains took Chief Hadley and Officer McKeon to the side of the pond where we'd seen the things in the water. The Chief peered down. So did McKeon. Lew Jarman and Mr. Beal joined them.

Finally Chief Hadley said, "There *is* something down there, so help me. Get ready, Mac."

McKeon stripped to a pair of bathing trunks and put on his skin-diving gear, which he had removed from the car. A few seconds later he was deep under water, bubbles streaming away from his mask. Nobody at the side of the pond said a word. We just watched McKeon swim around the car. Finally he got a handhold and then began tugging at the figure to get it loose.

My scalp tingled and my stomach squirmed.

At last Officer McKeon shot straight up. He was holding the thing. I turned away as he came to the surface. I couldn't look.

I heard a kind of funny gasp go up from Mr. Beal, who was standing beside me. Then, Officer McKeon called out.

"Well, he's stiff right enough."

Then, he laughed. *Laughed!!*

I turned around. I couldn't help myself. I saw everything in one quick glance. Officer McKeon was crawling out of the pond. He had tossed the "thing" on the stubbly grass. It was lying there, on its back, both arms spread wide.

But it wasn't a man. It wasn't any part of a human. It was one of those things that are used in store windows to display clothes. It was a mannequin—a dummy!

4 FINGER OF SUSPICION

I WENT NUMB. I JUST STOOD THERE, NOT BELIEVING WHAT I SAW. Brains wasn't in any better shape. He looked as if he'd been hit hard on the head and was about to drop.

Nobody said anything until Mr. Beal sort of gasped, "Well, what do you know—a dummy!"

Officer McKeon laughed again but Chief Hadley didn't. He swung his massive body around until he was facing Brains and me. His mouth was tight and there was a nasty light in his small eyes.

"O.K., Benton," he snapped. "And you, Carson. You've pulled your childish trick on me. And I won't forget it. I warn you, from now on stay out of my sight—and out of my business!"

Brains usually was able to control himself. But he wasn't now. His face was as red as a fireman's shirt and he was boiling mad.

"It was no trick!" he said. "We reported what we saw. You've got to admit that mannequin resembled a human body from up here. Anybody would've been fooled. You were, yourself."

"Bah!" Chief Hadley growled. "You talk too much. You're too big for your britches. If I were your father I'd put you in your place with a switch!"

The Chief lurched toward the police car.

"Change into your clothes, Mac," he snapped at Officer Mc-Keon. "And hurry! I've got to get back to my office. This stupid trip has given the thief who stole the Camp Fund that much more time to get away."

Lew Jarman took a casual step in Chief Hadley's direction. "Of course you'll have that car pulled out of the pool, won't you, Chief?" he said. "Might be interesting to find out who owns it—and why it was driven in there last night with a dummy passenger."

"Naturally, we'll raise it," Chief Hadley said quickly. I'll swear the idea hadn't crossed his mind until then. "What did you think, we'd leave it there?"

The Chief didn't invite Brains to ride back with him to town in the police car. And he didn't invite me, either. Lew Jarman took us in his. Mr. Beal came along too, of course.

On the way to Crestwood, the reporter and Harvey Beal got to discussing the robbery. They seemed to think that the job had been done by an amateur to judge from the crude way Mr. Beal's office had been entered and the safe opened. What bothered both men was that whoever stole the money must have known about the windup of the Camp Fund drive the previous night, which seemed to indicate that the guilty party was someone right in Crestwood.

"It doesn't seem possible that anybody in town would stoop so low as to steal that money," Harvey Beal said.

Brains and I just listened to the talk. He didn't speak one word all the way to town. Neither did I. We'd stuck our necks out far enough for one day.

Lew Jarman let us out at the corner of Maple and Franklin,

close to my house. Brains lived on Chestnut Drive, only a few blocks away.

"Cheer up, you guys," Lew said. "You did your duty. I agree with Mr. Beal here that there may be a connection between the sunken car and the stolen camp dough. Don't let the Chief get you down. He's not half as bad as he sounds. He just doesn't understand kids like you. That's all."

I had nothing to say to that. Nor had Brains. My partner was still smarting from the working over Chief Hadley had given us. And it took no crystal ball to figure out that he was now more determined than ever to make Crestwood's overweight police chief recognize our worth as detectives. It was like an unofficial declaration of war. Old fatso Hadley was in for a heap of surprises. That seemed certain. When you tangled with my pal Brains, it was like tangling with a buzz saw.

When Lew Jarman and Mr. Beal had driven off, Brains motioned me to him. He glanced suspiciously up and down the street and scanned the vacant lot behind us before he spoke.

"I am calling an emergency conference of the agency's personnel," he said, his voice lowered to a whisper. "Report to headquarters as soon as possible after lunch, Operative Three. Let nothing deter you."

"Operative Three will be there, X," I whispered back.

With that, we parted.

I'd better point out that when Brains and I were working on a case, we used cover names rather than our own, in the interest of security. Brains' cover name was X. And I was Operative Three. There was no actual Operative Two, although sometimes we spoke as if there were.

I scooted fast along Maple Street toward my family's house at number 43, knowing full well that I was plenty late for lunch. And I knew, too, that my mother's good humor, which I had counted on so heavily, had probably been soured by news of the Camp Fund robbery.

My clothes were dry by this time, but were they a mess. Somehow I'd have to make a complete change before facing Mom.

I managed to sneak unseen into the kitchen and I was stealing upstairs when, like a dope, I stepped on the one board that creaked.

"Is that you, Jimmy?" my mother called out from the front room.

Well, I was caught. When Mom saw me she let out a little shriek and threw up her hands.

"James MacDonald Carson," she said, "where on earth have you been?"

There was nothing to do but tell her everything, which I did —about Boiling Pond, the sunken car and the dummy, even to the theory that maybe all this was tied up in some way with the robbery. Mom heard me out. She was too upset over the Camp Fund's being swiped to be mad at me.

"It's a terrible thing, Jimmy," she said. "We worked so hard and people gave so freely. Some contributed more than they could really afford. And to think that it is all gone. . . . Now get upstairs and change your clothes, for goodness' sake. I'll warm up your lunch."

It didn't take me long to put on fresh things and I was back downstairs in no time. I polished off a plateful of ham and fried potatoes and a couple of glasses of milk. I was anxious to get to headquarters and hear if Brains had figured anything out.

"Sure tasted good, Mom," I said as I got up from the table. "Guess I'll go downtown and get the handlebars on my bike fixed."

"Before you do anything else, go to the butcher's and pick up the meat I ordered for supper," Mom said.

There were half a dozen people in the butcher shop when I

got there, all talking at once. It seemed that the news of the car in Boiling Pond had spread like a grass fire. I was standing there waiting my turn, when I heard of an exciting development.

"That could be Ben Carlin's car," a man told one of the butchers. "He reported it stolen to the police late this morning."

Creeps! Things were really happening.

Ben Carlin lived in Crestwood. He was nineteen and worked at the Acme Garage. I knew him well enough to say, "Hi, Ben." He usually kept his car in the lot back of the garage. But the important thing to me was that this lot was almost next door to Harvey Beal's real estate office where the robbery had taken place.

Bits of the puzzle suddenly seemed to fit together. I saw it this way: The crook breaks into Mr. Beal's office, swipes the fund money and leaves. He desperately needs a getaway car. He sees Ben's and takes it and drives it up to Boiling Pond where he has left his own car. The crook gets rid of Ben's car by driving it into the pond. Then he steps into his own car and vanishes.

As soon as I'd been given the meat Mom ordered, I lit out for Brains'. I couldn't wait to take the meat home and then come back. I had to talk to my partner right away.

It must have been close to half past two when I hurriedly wheeled my bike along the lane toward the Benton garage at the rear of their property. The garage had once been a coach house and was good-sized, with rooms on the second floor. Some time ago, Brains' father and mother had let their son take over these rooms to do what he liked with them.

And what Brains had done was fantastic. He'd turned the rooms into a super-modern workshop and crime laboratory. He had accumulated so much scientific apparatus, power tools and crime detection equipment that the place resembled the lair of a mad scientist in a horror movie plus the control room of a space ship.

It was here that the Benton and Carson International Detective Agency maintained its secret headquarters.

Entrance could be made to the crime lab solely by a complicated system known only to Brains and me. First, a secret contact point had to be pressed on the outside of the garage. Then, the correct password for that day had to be spoken. When this was done, a panel in the wall of the garage slid open. You stepped through into a darkened cubicle where a staircase led upward. You mounted this staircase, which immediately began to fold up after you. At the top another door opened and you were in the laboratory.

I now followed this procedure, after first carefully checking that no one was spying on me, like Mrs. Ray, the Bentons' housekeeper. Brains was pacing up and down when I arrived. He was wearing his white lab coat and looked very professional.

"I had expected you earlier, Operative Three," he said, "until I became aware that you had been commissioned to go to the butcher's."

"How did you figure that?" I asked.

Brains shrugged. "Elementary. I watched your approach from the lookout with my binoculars. I noted two dogs almost knocked you off your bicycle. They seemed most interested in that package you're carrying." He paused and sniffed. "Lamb has a distinct odor. Also, there is sawdust on your shoes. A butcher shop is just about the only place you could have been."

"Bull's-eye," I said. "Now let me tell you something."

Brother, I could hardly wait to spring my news on him.

"You mean about Ben Carlin's car being stolen last night?" Brains asked.

I felt like a balloon must when it meets up with a sharp pin.

"Yeah!" I let out. "How come you know about that?"

"I got my short wave radio fixed a while ago. The police calls come in nicely."

I sat down on a bench. "Well, then," I said, "I've got something else to tell you—I think I've doped out how the robbery was pulled."

"*Modus operandi*," Brains said.

I glanced at him sharply. I didn't know what it meant but I didn't like the sound of it.

"Relax, Operative Three," Brains said. "The phrase means simply 'a method of working.' Proceed with your theory."

I did, ending up with, "And for my money Ben Carlin's car being swiped cinches the connection between the robbery and what we found at Boiling Pond."

Brains had the fingers of both hands pressed tightly together in front of him. He looked over them at me.

"There are a number of holes in your reconstruction of the crime," he said, quietly. "First, we are not certain that the car at the bottom of the pond *is* Ben Carlin's. Second, why would a thief making away with his haul pause to get hold of a display mannequin and place it in the car?"

I scratched my head. "Maybe he stole the car first and put the dummy in it so it would look as if somebody was in the car while the robbery was going on."

"Interesting idea but unnecessarily complicated," Brains said. "Also, it seems rather ridiculous for the robber or robbers to ditch the car in Boiling Pond when they could have simply abandoned it almost anywhere."

I put my head in my hands. The theory that had seemed so hot now was as cold as a left-over sardine.

"So what do we do?" I asked sarcastically. "Just sit here?"

Brains commenced his pacing again.

"Not at all. Our first move, Operative Three, is to check on one of the principal figures in this case."

"Like who?" I asked.

"Like the mannequin—the dummy," he replied.

"Huh? A lot that thing'll tell us."

"It may tell us much more than you think," Brains said. He seemed excited now and his eyes were blinking. "Yes, we must find out where the dummy came from—who owned it. That means returning to Boiling Pond."

He held up both hands, palms outward, as I started to protest.

"Not this afternoon, Operative Three. Tomorrow morning. And we shall not rendezvous here in case this place has been put under observation. Our meeting place will be the school bus shelter at Todd's Hill. Time: eight-thirty a.m., sharp."

"Got it," I said. Some of Brains' excitement began coming off on me.

"One more thing," Brains said. "Be positive you are not followed."

My father was home when I got there. He was head accountant at the gas works and sometimes he was able to get off a little early. I soon found out that he knew all about the incident at Boiling Pond. In fact, I gathered that the story of how Brains and I had discovered the sunken car and the body and called in Chief Hadley had swept back and forth across town like wildfire. From what my dad said, just about everybody was ribbing Chief Hadley over his part in recovering the "body." The Chief wasn't taking it too gracefully.

My dad wasn't as mad at me as I had expected. He seemed almost amused. I was grateful for that.

"I know you and Benton did what you thought best, Jimmy," my father said. "But from here on in, try to stay out of trouble."

"Yes, sir," I said. "I'll try."

Mom came in from the kitchen just then. "I suppose there've

been no new developments in the robbery, John," she said.

"I sure haven't heard of anything," Pop said.

But there had been a development in the case. We heard about it while we were eating supper. The radio was on and we were listening to music when all of a sudden the program was interrupted.

"This is a special bulletin," the local announcer said. "Chief George Hadley of the Crestwood Police Department has just announced the detention of a suspect in the theft of the Crestwood Community Camp Fund money. A witness whose identity is withheld has placed the suspect at the scene of the crime. The name of the suspect has been given as that of Will Parslow of this city."

"Will Parslow!" Mom was so startled she dropped her fork.

"That's crazy!" my dad said. "Will would never do a thing like that."

I was just as flabbergasted. Brains' old friend was the last person on earth to pull that robbery. It was plain nuts. Old Chief Hadley had fallen over his feet again.

Then, I remembered something and a chill came over me. It had been Mr. Parslow who had pointed out Boiling Pond to Brains only a few weeks ago. And Boiling Pond had been the place where the probable getaway car had been dumped. Putting two and two together, it didn't look good. Not good at all for the town's tinkerer and handyman, Will Parslow.

5 VITAL EVIDENCE

IN THE MORNING WHEN WE SAT DOWN TO BREAKFAST, MY MOTHER said, "I still can't believe it."

"The police wouldn't make an arrest unless they're pretty sure, Clara," my dad told her.

I stayed out of the conversation. I was too busy downing my oatmeal.

"Stop gulping your food, Jimmy!" Mom said.

"Yes'm." I looked at the clock. It was nearly eight-fifteen. Brains was really a nut for being on time.

"Well, I'd better get going," my dad said. "Sure hope they're wrong about Will."

Just about everybody in Crestwood liked Will Parslow. Of course, there were those who thought of him as shiftless. And maybe he was. At one time he'd had a little repair shop on Spruce Street. But now he just did odd jobs. He could make or fix anything.

That was how Brains and he had met. Both of them were the inventor type and they each knew what the other one was talking about. Brains had respect for the older man's intelligence and ability. More than once I'd known Brains to take some gadget or apparatus he was stumped with to Will Parslow. And Mr. Parslow had done the job.

Brains and the old man had even worked out some inventions together. Like that new-fangled fishing rod with a kind of automatic reel or something they'd tried out at Lake Carmine. Brains sure was going to be upset when he heard the news of the arrest.

And Mrs. Parslow was just about the kindest woman in Crestwood outside of my mother. Any kid happening by her house could be sure of a couple of her ginger cookies.

I felt sorry for the Parslows' kids. Johnny was in the class behind me in school. Gracie was in the second grade.

"I'm going to go over to see Ella Parslow soon as I get the dishes washed," my mother said. "She'll need somebody right now."

Dad said that was the thing to do. It was a break for me. With all this excitement I hoped my mother would forget to ask me what I was going to be up to today. That's just what she did.

Even so, I was a little late when I got to the school bus shelter about two miles out of town. I hadn't been followed, I was sure.

Brains consulted his wristwatch and said, "Not bad, Operative Three."

I noticed that he had one of his cameras strapped to him.

"I guess you heard about Will Parslow," I said.

"Of course!" Brains spoke as if the subject was distasteful.

We got on our bikes and headed for Boiling Pond.

"I wonder who the mysterious witness is who put the finger on him," I said. "But Chief Hadley is sure to keep that under cover for a while yet."

"I know already," Brains said.

"You do!"

"Stony Rhodes called to see me last night," Brains went on. "His job as a copy boy at the *Ledger* brings him into contact with certain information. The identity of the witness was known at the newspaper office. So, Stony relayed it on to me."

I suddenly saw red. All anybody had to do was mention Stony's name to me and I went up in flames. I loathed that character. We'd never got along and we never would if I had anything to do with it.

I mentioned Stony a while back. He was the kid who was standing at the curb when Brains and I drove past in the Chief's police car. He had yellow hair and a stupid giggle and he was always trying to join our detective agency. This was another prime example of his sneaky way—using his summer job as a copy boy to slip into Brains' good graces.

"You mean you took *that* guy's word, Brains?" I said.

Brains shrugged. "Why not? Lots of detectives use stool pigeons. And he happened to be telling the truth. The person who caused Mr. Parslow's arrest is Sarah Pruett."

That surprised but didn't shock me. Mrs. Pruett, or the Widow Pruett as she was known in town, was a peevish old number with a face that would've looked just dandy on a prune.

"Do you know anything about her testimony?" I asked.

"Only that she claims she was sitting at her window late the night before last, knitting, and she saw Will Parslow in Harvey Beal's office," Brains said.

The Widow Pruett lived above her stationery store downtown. Her place was just across an areaway from the building where Harvey Beal's office was. She was always sitting at her window and knitting. Somebody had once said that she reminded him of Madame Defarge in Dickens' *Tale of Two Cities*.

"What's Mr. Parslow got to say?" I asked.

Brains shook his head grimly. "He denies he was in Beal's office. He claims he took a two-mile hike that night to give an estimate on a house-painting job up near Bleeker City. But when he got there the people weren't home. And apparently nobody saw him going or coming back."

"No alibi," I said.

"Not one that'll hold water anyway," Brains said. "I'm confident that Mr. Parslow is completely innocent but I'll admit the circumstances against him are, at the moment, formidable."

We stood up on the pedals to make the big hill going past Woodward's truck farm.

"But, Brains," I said, "if the Widow Pruett claims she saw Mr. Parslow in that office, it seems that she must have. Why would she make up a story like that?"

I noticed that Brains' hands went tight on the handlebars until the knuckles showed white.

"She hates Will Parslow," he said. "You may not remember the trouble that broke out between those two a few years back. Mrs. Pruett swore then she'd have her revenge on Mr. Parslow."

All of a sudden I did recall the business that Brains was talking about. It had happened in the winter. The Widow Pruett was famous for her stinginess and she refused to hire anybody to keep her sidewalk free of snow and ice. One day Will Parslow slipped on the ice in front of her store and fell. He broke a leg or something. Anyway, he sued the widow and she finally had to pay damages. It almost killed her. She would rather eat a goat than part with a dollar.

We rode on in silence for a while. Then I said, "Brains, there's one thing that sort of worries me."

"What's that?" he asked.

I hesitated. "Well, it has to do with Mr. Parslow showing you Boiling Pond just a couple of weeks ago."

"I know what you mean, Jimmy," Brains said, soberly. "It

bothers me, also—very much, in fact."

We came to where the old woods road was. It was too rugged for our bikes, so we hid them in the bushes and went the rest of the way on foot.

The place seemed even spookier to me than when I'd first seen it. I guess that was because it held a secret.

The store dummy was where Officer McKeon had thrown it. We both examined it. It had a man's face painted on it. The paint had chipped badly. Brains took a picture of the thing.

"Looks to me as if this mannequin was thrown out long ago," Brains said. "I only hope Mr. Porter will recognize it from this picture."

Mr. Porter owned the leading haberdashery in town. I'd got my blue serge suit there.

Brains was about to take another shot when we both heard something. It wasn't very loud at first, but it stepped up fast.

"It's a truck! Coming in here!" Brains said. "Hide!"

We both headed for cover back of a big boulder and fell flat. The roar got louder each second, and for a minute I wondered if the army had picked out this place to test a new tank.

We kept down. Then the monster came out in full view. It was a big construction truck pulling a big crane with a hook on the end. The driver had a bad time swinging it around so that the derrick hung out over the pond. A few minutes later a police car arrived. Chief Hadley and Officer McKeon stepped out and walked to the edge of the pond. McKeon had his skin-diving equipment again.

"He'll have to go down and hook the car on," Brains whispered.

"He can have the job," I said.

"That's a Scotch derrick," Brains said in my ear, knowing everything as usual. "It can lift a great deal of weight. The only trouble with it is you can't slew it around in a full circle."

"I'll remember that when I buy one," I said.

Officer McKeon dropped into the pond and swam around for a few moments while they dropped the big hook into the water. He guided it to the right spot, signaled for the men on the big truck to lower it, then disappeared beneath the surface.

It was quite a sight, that big crane lifting the car out of Boiling Pond.

"It's Ben Carlin's old heap right enough," I said, when it was unhooked from the crane. "He put that coat of dark green paint on it a couple of weeks ago."

At that moment a tow car with Acme Garage lettered on the side drove up. When the driver hopped out I was surprised to see that it was Ben Carlin, himself. I shouldn't have been surprised really. After all, Ben did work at the Acme Garage.

Ben hurried over to where Chief Hadley was gazing at the car that had been brought up from the depths. We couldn't hear what Ben or the Chief said, for the construction truck was making a terrific noise as it began to tug the big crane away. But, obviously, Chief Hadley was asking Ben if this was his car and Ben was nodding.

Ben was a tall, big-shouldered guy and it seemed like he always needed a haircut. If he'd had a bigger nose he would have looked like a young Abe Lincoln. He'd been born and raised in Crestwood and he'd been pretty famous as a football player a couple years back when he'd attended Crestwood High.

But according to my dad and to others, Ben would never be as famous as his father had been. Ben's father hadn't played football. He'd been a racing-car driver and one of the best. He'd won all sorts of races and set many records. Then, around ten years ago, I think, he'd been killed in a pile-up at the annual Columbus Day Road Race at Middlebury. To make matters worse, not long after that, Ben's mother had died—and Ben had gone to live with his uncle, Sam Lufkin, who lived in the south part of Crestwood. Mr. Lufkin was a bachelor and retired. He did his best to raise Ben, and Ben did his best to be nice to his uncle. But it was a strain for both.

What made it doubly hard was that just before Ben's mother died, she made Sam Lufkin swear that he would never let young Ben in a racing car. She made him swear it on the Bible, my dad said. So Sam Lufkin was forever checking up on Ben and quizzing him as to where he'd been and all.

All this happened when I was a little kid. So, all the dope I had on Ben was mostly second hand. But I did remember when Ben refused to go on to college and took a job at the Acme Garage. He said then that all he wanted to do was work on cars. And that's exactly what he'd done.

The big construction truck had by now reached the woods road with the crane in tow. And pretty soon the heavy equipment was out of sight and out of hearing. Brains and I remained where we were behind the big boulder. By peering around the sides through the heavy weeds, we could watch what went on without much fear of detection.

Chief Hadley and Officer McKeon were going over Ben's recovered car with great care. Ben was standing close by, watching.

"The one night I left the keys in the car," he said, "that would be the time when somebody took a notion to steal it."

"You had it insured, of course," we heard Chief Hadley say.

Ben nodded. "Oh, sure."

Officer McKeon brought something out from the back seat of the car and handed it to the Chief. It was a brief case.

"Beal said the fund money was in one," Brains whispered.

"Sh-h-h-h-h!" I said.

"Been cut open with a knife," Chief Hadley said. "It sure had to have a big blade."

I shivered. Will Parslow often wore a big knife in a sheath at his belt. He liked to whittle.

Chief Hadley took Ben over to where the mannequin lay. Officer McKeon was examining it closely.

"That's what you pulled out of the car yesterday?" Ben said. "This sure is crazy."

"Looks worse for Parslow all the time," the Chief said. "Well, let's get back to town."

Ben Carlin hooked up his soaking wet car to the Acme Garage tow car. Then, slowly, he headed away down the woods road. The police car bearing Chief Hadley and Officer McKeon followed, leaving that old dummy lying there staring at the sky.

When they were out of sight, we came from behind the boulder and lost no time in legging it to where we'd parked our bikes.

We intended to make our first stop at Mr. Porter's men's store when we got into town, but Brains changed our plans.

"We haven't seen Mr. Beal's office yet," he said. "I don't think the police will let him put it to rights until they've sifted it for all clues that might be there."

We parked our bikes at the curb and went up the long flight of steps to Mr. Beal's real estate office on the second floor. Brains was a little ahead of me. When he reached the top of the stairs, he suddenly gestured to me for silence.

I didn't know what was up. I noticed that the door to Mr. Beal's office was partly open and that Brains was stealing a look inside. I sneaked up beside him and took a look, too. And I got a real shock.

Chief Hadley was in there, talking to Mr. Beal. Or, rather, it was Harvey Beal who was doing most of the talking.

"You've had time to search the place inch by inch a dozen times, Chief," the real estate man was saying indignantly. "I've got business to attend to. I've got to get this mess cleaned up."

From the brief view I could get of the inside, the office sure did look a mess. The drawers of a filing cabinet were pulled out and their contents had been scattered on the floor. A waste-paper basket had been tipped over. And the small office safe stood across the room, its door hanging open.

"Now, Harv," Chief Hadley said importantly, "there still may be important clues here which have been overlooked. You must leave everything as it is until my experts have completed their investigation."

I tugged at Brains' sleeve. "Let's beat it," I said.

"All in good time," he whispered back.

I thought for a moment he was going to barge into Mr. Beal's office and confront Chief Hadley. Perhaps he was. If so, he changed his mind and motioned for me to go back down the stairs. Which I did. I was real anxious to put space between old fatso Hadley and us.

Brains was taking an unholy amount of time coming down the stairs. I noticed that he had his head down and was inspecting every step. All of a sudden he took out his handkerchief and bent over. He picked up something, placed it carefully in his handkerchief, then slipped the handkerchief into his pocket.

"What did you find?" I asked when we were out on the street.

"Just a piece of earth," Brains said. "Most people, when they talk about an H-bomb dropping, Operative Three, think only of where it hits. They neglect to take the fall-out into consideration."

"Clear as mud," I said. He can be awfully tormenting at times.

"Let's hope this piece of dried mud will be clearer," Brains murmured.

He plunged off with that long-legged walk of his, leaving me standing there with my mouth hanging open. I headed for home in a complete fog.

6 STRANGE MENACE

WHEN I REPORTED TO THE CRIME LAB AFTER LUNCH, I FOUND Brains bent over a microscope.

"This is most interesting, Operative Three," he said without looking up.

I saw that he was inspecting the hunk of dirt he'd picked up on the stairs.

"What's the dope?" I asked.

"It came from a shoe, I'm positive. From between the heel and the sole. . . . What do you make of this?"

Brains dropped three small objects in the palm of my hand. They were old squash or pumpkin seeds.

"They were caked in with the dirt," he said. "I also found this in it."

He handed me a piece of thin wire with some of the insulation still clinging to it. It was about a quarter of an inch long.

"It doesn't mean a thing to me," I said.

"You are not very observing today," Brains said. "You will notice these seeds are more than dry. They're dead."

He picked up some of the dirt and told me to smell it.

I sniffed at it. I had to admit I'd never smelled dirt like it. It had an odor of decay and made me shiver. It reminded me of a picture I'd seen at the Cameo a few days before: *Daughter of Dracula.*

I knew now what Brains had meant by folks overlooking the fall-out. Chief Hadley and his men hadn't looked very far from the scene of the robbery.

Brains carefully picked the portions of dirt up with tweezers and dropped the stuff into a small glass jar.

"We'll continue our investigation of this later," he said. "Our next step is a visit to the haberdasher's."

It seemed that Brains had already printed the photograph he'd taken of the dummy. So we went downtown and showed it to Mr. Porter at his store. He recognized the dummy right away.

"Why, yes," he said, "that display mannequin was mine. But I gave it away some time ago. It was very old and in disrepair. I can't afford to have anything run-down in an up-to-date establishment like this."

"No, indeed," Brains said. "Do you remember who you gave the figure to, Mr. Porter?"

"Why, yes," Mr. Porter said, "to that Will Parslow fellow. He told me he might be able to fix it up. I said he could try but to throw the thing away if the repairs would cost me more'n a dollar. I suppose he threw it away."

I groaned inwardly. It sure looked bad for Mr. Parslow.

I don't think I'd ever seen Brains more discouraged than when we left Mr. Porter's store.

"The case against Will Parslow couldn't be much blacker," he said. "Everything seems to be stacked against him. Yet, I know he's innocent. It would be almost impossible for a man of his make-up to steal money. Money doesn't mean that much to him. If it did, he'd have a good job. No, Will Parslow is an honest man."

"Yeah," I said, "but saying it is one thing and proving it is another."

Brains turned and gripped me tightly by the arm. "Jimmy," he said intensely, "you have just stated a truth. We must prove Mr. Parslow's innocence. We must save him."

"O.K.," I said. I was about to ask how when Brains cut me off.

"Then, you're in complete agreement that the facilities of the Benton and Carson International Detective Agency be thrown into this case?" he asked.

"Yeah," I said. "Sure. I guess so."

"I knew I could count on you, Operative Three," Brains exclaimed. "Our campaign will be daring and bold. Our next move is obvious."

"Not to me, it isn't," I said.

Brains had already started down the street.

"Where're we going?" I called after him.

"To jail," my partner said. "To confer with our client, Will Parslow."

Well, I went along. But I'm telling you I dragged my feet all the way. I could imagine what Chief Hadley would say and what he would do when he heard we wanted to talk to Mr. Parslow. I had a vision of the two of us being heaved bodily into the street.

But, believe it or not, nothing like that happened. I think that Chief Hadley was just too stunned to object when Brains walked into the police station and stated that we had come to see the suspect in the Community Camp Fund robbery case and that it was illegal to hold any prisoner incommunicado.

Anyway, presto, we were taken back to the row of cells at the rear of the station house. The cells were all vacant except Mr. Parslow's.

Will Parslow was a frail-looking man, middle-aged, with a wrinkled, kindly face. Now, seeing him behind bars, he seemed even frailer. And he was scared. You could tell.

But was he happy to see Brains!

"I'm so glad you've come, Benton, my boy," he said. "Please try to explain to somebody that a dreadful mistake has been made. I didn't steal any money."

"I know you didn't," Brains said. "That's why we're here. We intend to get you your freedom. But first, I must have certain information."

"I'll tell you anything," Mr. Parslow said. "Anything."

There were some chairs in the corridor outside Mr. Parslow's cell and Brains and I sat down. A uniformed policeman was at a desk down at the end of the corridor doing some paper work. I guess he kept an eye on us to see that we didn't slip anything to the prisoner through the bars. But other than that we were left alone.

"I understand you stated that on the night of the crime you took a two-mile hike to give an estimate on a house-painting job," Brains said.

"That's true," Mr. Parslow said. "I went to see Mr. and Mrs. Vernay. They live just this side of Bleeker City."

Brains removed a notebook from his pocket and wrote something in it. I envied him. He looked so professional.

"And Mr. and Mrs. Vernay were not at home when you got there?" Brains said.

"Correct," Will Parslow said. "I waited around for a while and then struck out for home."

"How long did you wait?"

"Twenty minutes. Maybe half an hour."

"Hmmmmm," Brains murmured. He tapped the end of his pencil against his teeth. "Don't you usually whittle things with your knife when you have time on your hands?"

"That I do," Mr. Parslow said.

"Did you happen to do any whittling the night you waited for the Vernays to return?"

Will Parslow's eyes got wide. "Why, I did. I sat there on the edge of the veranda and I cut out a whistle for my boy."

"The chips from that whittling may still be there," Brains said. He glanced meaningly at me. "What kind of wood was it, Mr. Parslow?"

"Willow," Will Parslow said without hesitation.

"And what happened to the whistle? Did you complete it? Did you give it to your son?"

"I finished it and I gave it to Johnny. He should still have it."

"I hope so," Brains said. "That whistle may prove to be an important piece of evidence."

I was wondering if my partner was going to skip asking Mr. Parslow about the dummy. But I should've known better. Brains waited until we'd got to our feet and were about to leave. Then he produced the photograph of the dummy and showed it to Mr. Parslow.

"Ever see this before, sir?" Brains asked, casually.

Mr. Parslow put on his reading glasses and examined the picture.

"Good gracious, yes!" he exclaimed. "That's the display figure Mr. Porter gave me a couple of months ago! Why on earth have you a picture of it?"

Either Mr. Parslow didn't know about Ben Carlin's car being found at the bottom of the pool with the dummy in it or he was putting on one peachy act.

"The mannequin may have a part in this case," Brains said and let it go at that. "What I'd like to find out now is what you did with this figure."

"I tried to mend it," Will Parslow said. "But it wasn't worth the trouble. So one day I just threw it out."

I noticed Brains take a deep breath. Then he said, "Do you recall the place where you discarded it?"

Mr. Parslow frowned. "Well, now," he said, "I don't rightly . . . Wait a minute! I do. I remember now. I was driving that old pickup truck I had then. I was on my way up to Lake Carmine for some fishing. I stopped off at Boiling Pond. Like we did the time you were with me, Benton. As I got out to eat a sandwich and wash it down with that cool spring water, I happened to see that wax figure lying in the back of the truck. I'd been meaning to get rid of it. So I did. I picked it up and threw it away."

Brains' eyes were batting fast as a hummingbird's wings.

"Just where did you throw it?" Brains asked sharply.

"I tossed it behind some rocks, seems like," Mr. Parslow said. "Up there on the north side of the pond. . . . Now what's this all about, boy? Why are you giving me the third degree over a beat-up store dummy?"

Brains didn't answer that one. Instead, he said, "As I understand it, you discarded the mannequin at Boiling Pond prior to the time you and I stopped by the Pond. Is that correct?"

"Yes, Benton, that's correct," Mr. Parslow said. "I wish I knew what you're getting at."

"Just this," Brains said. "If this mannequin was lying discarded close to Boiling Pond before our visit, why didn't I see it when I was there?"

Mr. Parslow still appeared perplexed. But his answer was forthright enough.

"Naturally, you wouldn't have seen it, my boy. We stayed at the south side of the pond, remember? And as I said before, I threw the figure behind the rocks on the north side."

"True," Brains said. And he began to smile a little as if a load of worry had just been lifted. "Very true."

Then, Brains shook hands with Mr. Parslow and we left.

As we were walking down the street from the police station, Brains began humming *The Farmer in the Dell*. He always did when he was happy. Why he picked on that nursery rhyme, goodness only knows.

"I am at last seeing a ray of light through the darkness," he said to me.

"Huh?" I said.

"I'm convinced that it was used as a red herring," he said.

I glanced at him out of the corner of my eye. Sometimes my partner acted pretty goofy. This was one of those times.

"I mean, Operative Three," Brains went on, "that the mannequin was probably placed in Ben Carlin's car just before it was run into the pond to confuse the authorities. And nothing more."

I was chewing on that one when Brains spoke again.

"There is one thing you must do," he said. "Obtain your parents' permission to sleep out the next couple of nights in the tent in my yard. You might stress the healthful qualities of fresh air for growing youth. But how you argue your case will be up to you. Only don't fail. It is essential for us to have freedom of movement without parental objections."

"O.K.," I said. It would take some selling but I felt I could put it over.

Right about then, who should we meet but Ben Carlin.

"I hear it was you two sleuths who spotted my car in Boiling Pond," Ben said. "I'm mighty obliged to you. I guess you're scouting around for clues to who swiped it, huh? And who got away with all that money."

"We're interested," Brains said, flatly.

Ben Carlin acted sort of excited about something. "Look what I found just now in the lot back of the garage where I kept my car. I'm taking it to the police."

It was a book of matches. Brains and I read the printing on it: *LeDore's Tavern. Good Food. Bridgefield.*

"That's nearly a hundred miles from here," I said.

"The thief must've dropped it," Ben said.

Brains handed the book of matches back to Ben Carlin. "Maybe," he sort of grunted. "Let's go, Jimmy."

"You've got to admit it's a possibility," I said after we'd left Ben.

"Didn't it rain heavily early this morning?" Brains asked me. "Wasn't there thunder and lightning, too?"

"That's right. It woke me up."

"When it rains on a book of matches all the sulphur tips get glued together," Brains said. "The matches in the book Ben said he'd just found in the parking lot were in perfect shape. That book, therefore, couldn't have been dropped at the time his car was stolen."

"Gosh," I said. "I guess you're right."

We went to the crime lab and Brains parked himself in his "thinking chair" and thought. After a while he said, "We must visit the Vernays' place before we go on with the rest of the night's work."

I had a hunch he was thinking of Boiling Pond when he spoke of night's work. And I wasn't too enthusiastic.

"Bring your blankets to the tent around seven o'clock, Jimmy," Brains said.

"Will do," I said, hopefully.

My mother took a dim view of my sleeping outdoors. But not my dad. He said it was healthy. He said he was sorry he couldn't do it any more. He went into such a spiel about how he'd spent the best summers he'd had as a kid camping outdoors and sleeping in a tent that I didn't have to whip up any sales talk at all.

After supper, I carried my bedroll over to Brains' and dumped it on a cot in the tent he'd put up back of the house. Mrs. Ray, the housekeeper, watched me from the back door.

"If you ask me," she said, "children should be kept indoors at night, under lock and key. No good will come of giving them all this freedom. No good. Mark my words."

Brains was sitting on his camp cot and he yawned as the housekeeper's shrill voice came through the canvas sides of the tent.

"Creeps," I said. "Isn't she liable to get your parents all stirred up, carrying on like that?"

Brains shook his head. "No great danger," he said. "Anyway, both my mother and father happen to be at a meeting at the college. . . . Now, come along. The Vernays await our visit."

The Vernays turned out to be a nice couple. But they hadn't told Will Parslow they were going to have their house painted. So somebody else must have told him. Yes, Mrs. Vernay said, she'd swept up some whittlings from the veranda but she'd tossed them into the fire.

"Too bad," Brains said. "It might have helped to save Will Parslow. You would testify though that you did find willow whittlings?"

"Whittlings, yes," Mrs. Vernay said, "but I couldn't swear they came off a willow stick."

"Thanks, Ma'am," Brains said, and we left.

A half hour later it was getting dark and there was a light mist over everything. We had to switch our bike lights on. The moon was just a thin crust of yellow bread in the sky. All we could hear was a dog howling quite a way off.

"It sure is dark to go poking around in any woods," I said.

"That's so," Brains said.

We rode for some time before we finally came to the old woods road leading to Boiling Pond. We ditched our bikes. It was so dark in the woods you could taste it.

"I don't see any sense in groping around where you can't see anything," I said.

"Criminals sometimes return to the scene of a crime, especially if they've hidden something close by," Brains said.

In the blackness we somehow got all turned around and we lost our way. We never got to the pond. After pushing through the woods for what seemed like hours, we came out of a clump of bushes and onto a graveled road. It had hardly been used since the new highway went through. It was the old road to Lake Carmine. I saw something loom up out of the mist ahead and suddenly knew where we were. It was exactly where I didn't want to be. My teeth started rattling.

Brains recognized the old chimney, too. It was all that was left standing of what my folks had told me was the old Gault house. There'd been a murder committed there and it had burned down over ten years ago. The ruins were partly hidden by weeds and small bushes.

"I've got butterflies doing barrel rolls in my stomach," I told Brains.

My heart was beating like bongo drums and I felt as if something was following us.

Even Brains got chicken. "I'd prefer looking this place over in daylight if it becomes necessary," he said. "It is a little too foggy for reconnoitering tonight. We'd better postpone our investigations until—"

Then we heard it.

It was like a strong wind coming up quick and roaring through the branches overhead. It stopped, then started again. We flattened out at the side of the road.

"A plane somewhere overhead," Brains whispered. "They sound that way on a quiet night. The engines fade out, then become loud again."

The sound came again. It lasted for only about two seconds. I was sure it didn't come from overhead. Nor from the woods. It seemed to come from under the ground.

Brains got up. "Come on, Operative Three. We haven't got the right to be detectives if we let every noise we hear scare us."

"You kiddin', Brains? You mean you're going nearer to that house?"

"Yes. There must be an explanation."

"Maybe. But I don't want to find out after I'm dead."

We crept nearer. There was a high bank along the edge of the road and we stuck close to it. Our feet sank into soft sand, which made the going quieter. The gravel in the center of the road crunched with every step.

We were almost opposite the ruins when we came to a big pile of old lumber and broken farm machinery heaped against the bank. Brains started around it and I was right behind him.

Then, before I could stop, something sticking out of that junk-pile caught on my jacket and clattered to the road. In the stillness it made an awful racket. I stood there, not breathing, not moving, not anything!

"What are you trying to do, wake the dead?" Brains hissed at me. Leave it to good old X to say the right thing at the right time.

"Don't you think this is far enough?" I whispered.

It sure was. I hadn't taken another step when the terrible sound split through the night. It was an agonizing groan that sent our skin crawling and glued our feet to the ground.

I never heard anything like it. If we'd been in Ireland I'd swear it was a banshee. It was like a soul in torment and the horrible sound lowered and fell like a March wind.

I got going first. Brains didn't catch up with me until a half mile later. *Creeps!*

7 MYSTERIOUS NOTE

WHEN WE RODE INTO CRESTWOOD WE HAD MOST OF OUR WITS back. At least, Brains did.

"I still don't believe in ghosts," he said.

"Neither do I, Brains, but I'm scared of 'em."

We agreed to say nothing about what happened out there. If we sent the police on another wild-goose chase they'd probably lock us up.

In the tent we undressed in the dark. Just before I fell asleep Brains said, "Maybe a freak of nature out there caused a wind tunnel somewhere, Jimmy. But I still think somebody tried to scare us away."

"It wasn't mice," I mumbled.

When I went home for breakfast the next morning, my dad asked me how I felt.

"Like a top," I told him, and it was no fib. I was still spinning a little.

There was a copy of yesterday's *Ledger* on the table. The headlines said: CITIZENS ASK FOR SWIFT JUSTICE. Parslow Still Denies Guilt After Stiff Cross-Examination. Held for Grand Jury.

"Can they send him to prison if they don't ever find the money, Dad?" I asked.

"I'm not sure, Jimmy. But as long as he lives around here he'll be a marked man."

"Gosh," I said.

"Most folks think there was more than one robber," my mother said. "One had to be a lookout and stay in the car."

I stayed clear of all such talk, believe me.

Brains was banging away at his typewriter, and just glanced at me over his glasses when I walked into the crime lab at eight-thirty.

"I shall be with you in a few moments, Operative Three," he said. "I must record in my case book what has transpired so far."

Brains had scheduled a visit to the Parslows' house. So ten minutes later we rode out there. It was a run-down clapboard house but real neat inside. Mrs. Parslow was frying doughnuts. She told us to help ourselves and we did. Her eyes looked like she'd been crying, but she smiled at us.

"We're quite convinced that Mr. Parslow is innocent," Brains said. "Our agency is making every effort to free him, Ma'am."

"You are two fine boys," Mrs. Parslow said, just as Johnny came in.

Brains asked him about the whistle.

"It didn't work very well," Johnny said. "I chucked it in the river yesterday."

Brains made a face. "It's probably floated out of the state by this time. Too bad, it might have helped, Mrs. Parslow."

"That whittling business? They wouldn't have believed it anyway," Mrs. Parslow said.

"Well, sorry to have bothered you, Ma'am," Brains said, "but we can't allow ourselves to overlook the slightest detail."

On our way back to the lab we passed the Acme Garage. Ben Carlin was just getting out of a beat-up car as we turned in.

"See you've got another car," Brains said.

"If you can call it that." Ben laughed. "I paid two hundred fifty for it."

"Cash?"

"Sure. The one that was stolen was insured for almost twice that much. My uncle advanced me the money because of the insurance I'm going to get from Mr. Beal." Ben kicked at one of the rear tires. "Looks like that one won't last very long."

When we got back to the lab, Brains picked up one of his cameras. It took a pretty good-sized picture. I didn't have to ask where we were going.

"I intend to find out if that ghost out there is diurnal as well as nocturnal, Operative Three," he said.

I could guess what he meant. But I didn't like returning to that scary place, even in the daytime. And I said so.

"Naturally there's an element of danger in our business," Brains said. "It is not a game of jacks."

"O.K.," I said. "Lead on."

We didn't have any trouble riding along the graveled road in broad daylight. The remains of the old Gault place didn't look too spooky this time. We found the spot where we'd climbed the bank the night before. Our tracks were there in the soft sand, but nobody else's. After Brains took a couple of pictures we walked as big as life through the ruins and up to the blackened chimney.

Creeps, was it quiet!

"That ghost must sleep in the daytime," I said.

We really combed that place but couldn't find where anything bigger than a woodchuck could hide.

"There is no sign that anyone has been here recently," Brains said. "The weeds haven't been trampled."

We examined the old cellar and turned over some chunks of masonry that had fallen from the foundation but there was nothing underneath but rotted grass and little crawling things.

"Well?" I said to Brains.

"I have to admit I am stumped at the moment," he said. "Perhaps we heard a giant screech owl last night."

"It had an awful cold if it was," I said.

Brains took more pictures and a sample of dirt from the old cellar. Then we returned to Crestwood.

Brains immediately got to work using his microscope. And it didn't take him long to find out that the dirt he found in the old cellar was nothing like the chunk he'd picked up on the steps leading to Mr. Beal's office.

It was my idea that we should knock off for a while and go down to Bennett's Drugstore for a Cherry-Fizz or a soda or something. Brains agreed. He said he'd stayed too close to the case and needed diversion.

Well, we'd barely left the Bentons' garage and were swinging along Chestnut Drive when we heard somebody yelling.

"Hey, stop! Stop!"

I looked around and groaned.

It was that pain in the neck, Stony Rhodes.

"Let's roll," I said urgently to Brains. "All he wants is to mess around in our business."

"Wait a minute," Brains said. He was staring back. "Stony seems to have something for us."

Stony had what looked to be a roll of paper in his hand. He was waving it frantically. Well, we waited and pretty soon the pest came galloping up. He was a thin-faced kid about five inches shorter than he should've been. His yellow hair was hanging down over his face and he was puffing like mad.

What he had in his hand was made of paper, all right—it was a newspaper, an early edition of the *Crestwood Daily Ledger*.

"I wanted you to see the big news," Stony gasped out, "before the papers hit the street. Look . . . look what's happened."

The story in the *Ledger* really knocked us for a loop. Early that morning a farmer out on a rural mail route between Crestwood and Middlebury had found a letter in his mailbox. There'd been no stamp on it. The letter had said:

> CHeeF OF POLiCe CRESTwOOd
> yOU gOt wROnG MAN
> w PARSLOw diDNt dO it

According to the newspaper the message hadn't been handwritten or typed. Instead, letters had been cut out of magazines and glued into place to spell out words. Some of the letters were bigger than the others. Some were colored and some were just black.

"That should clear Will Parslow," I said.

Brains shook his head. "On the contrary," he said. "People have been insisting right along that he had an accomplice. Now they'll say this letter was sent to confuse the D.A.'s case."

"Who do *you* think sent it?" I asked.

"Could be the work of a crank," Brains said.

Stony Rhodes had been keeping his trap closed. But now he opened it.

"When are you going to take me into your agency, Brains—er—Barclay?" he said. "I'm good at shadowing and watching people."

"Well, not yet, Stony," Brains said. "You must serve an apprenticeship in anything."

"That's right," I butted in. "Maybe as long as ten years."

Stony gave me a look that would have shriveled a raw pork chop. Then he left us.

Brains turned and started to walk back the way he had come.

"Where're you off to?" I asked.

"Stay where you are," he said. "I've got to get something at the lab. I'll rejoin you in a few minutes."

Sure enough, he was back in five.

"What'd you get?" I asked.

"It's of no consequence now," Brains said. "Follow me. We're going to the police station."

"Creeps! What for?" I kissed the Cherry-Fizz goodbye.

"I must see that anonymous note," Brains said.

"You'll see it over Chief Hadley's fat body," I said.

"Oh, he'll show it to us," Brains said mildly. "After all, our parents pay taxes. And taxes pay Chief Hadley's salary. I don't expect to be *given* the letter. I just want to look at it."

Of course, I went along. Good old Operative Three.

When we walked into the police station, Sergeant Hawkins took one look at us and let out a bellow.

"Beat it!" he said. "You can't see the Chief. He left strict orders about you two."

Lew Jarman, the *Daily Ledger* reporter, happened to come out of Chief Hadley's office at that moment. Brains went over and talked quietly to him. I couldn't hear what was said. But, a moment later, Lew Jarman went back into the Chief's office. In no time at all, he was out again.

"He'll see you," Lew said to Brains. "Go right in."

And we did.

"Now what do you want?" Chief Hadley asked icily.

"Oh, nothing much," Brains said, politely. "We'd just like to see that letter concerning Mr. Parslow."

The Chief's collar must have been too tight or something because his face got sort of swollen and red.

"Well, all right," he said. He kind of choked. "There it is."

He gestured to a side table. Lying on the table was the mysterious note. We went over and looked at it.

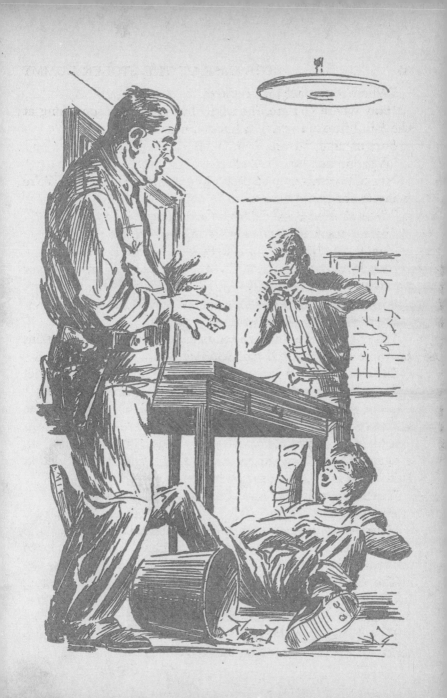

The note was just the way the newspaper had described it. Letters had been cut out and pasted on a piece of paper to form the words. They weren't all the same size and they were in a lot of different shapes and colors. Some were capitals and some were small letters, some stood up and others leaned over. Several had straight lines running across them.

While we were peering at the note, I noticed Chief Hadley go to the door of his office to say something to Sergeant Hawkins. Right then, Brains nudged me hard in the ribs with his elbow.

"Quick, make a diversion," Brains hissed. "Faint or something!"

I'd worked with Brains long enough not to ask questions, no matter how crazy his orders might sound.

I lurched to one side and fell over the wastebasket near the Chief's desk. Then I began howling like a wounded Apache Indian.

Chief Hadley came on the run. "What's wrong?" he yelled. "What's wrong?"

"Don't touch me," I yipped. "I might have a busted arm. Oh-h-h-h-h-h-h-h! Ow-w-w-w-w-w-w-w-w!"

Chief Hadley leaned over me as I writhed on the floor. He was joined by old Sergeant Hawkins.

"Phone for a doctor!" the Chief bellowed at the sergeant.

That was one person I didn't want. So I sat up. As I did so, I caught a glimpse of Brains. He had turned away from the table where the note was, stuffing something in his pocket. He winked in my direction, indicating that he'd finished whatever he'd wanted to do.

"There is no necessity to summon a doctor, Chief," Brains said. "I believe Jimmy feels all right now. He's subject to these fits."

"Fits?" Chief Hadley gasped.

Brains nodded. "The seizures are most mysterious. Run in his family. Only cases in medical history. I must get him home promptly."

Brains bent down and, taking me by the hand, pulled me to my feet.

"Come along, James," he said, soothingly. "Be calm now."

I leaned against him and tottered across the office to the door. I had to bite my lip to keep from laughing.

"Thank you so much for allowing us to inspect the note, sir," Brains said to Chief Hadley. "It has been a real privilege knowing you. . . . And you, too, Sergeant Hawkins."

The Chief and the sergeant had their mouths open but they didn't say a thing.

I waited until we were a block from the station house before asking Brains to come clean.

"What was the big idea?" I demanded. "What were you after?"

Brains smiled thinly. He took from his pocket his tiny candid camera.

"It was necessary for me to study that message closely," he said. "A photograph of it seemed to be the only answer. So, while you were dying there on the floor, I was able to make the shot unobserved. By the way, congratulations on your histrionic ability. You might go far on the stage."

Praise from Brains always set me up.

We'd almost reached the crime lab when I thought of something else.

"I don't get why old fatso Hadley didn't object to us peering at that note," I said. "Did Lew Jarman sort of smooth the way for us?"

Brains nodded. "Decidedly," he said. "You see, I anticipated Chief Hadley might refuse my request. So I suggested to Lew Jarman that he might remind the Chief that my father frequently writes Mayor Worthington's speeches. Apparently Chief Hadley got the point."

"Which was?" I said.

"Which was that as long as the present Mayor is in office, Chief Hadley can be reasonably certain of his job," Brains said.

"Politics!" I let out. "Don't you stop at anything?"

Brains raised his shoulders and lowered them in an expressive shrug.

"Not when a man's liberty is at stake," he said.

8 THE ATTACK

It was close to suppertime but I stuck around the lab while Brains developed the film and printed the shot he'd taken of the mystery note.

The picture came out fine, with the letters of the note showing up sharp and clear. While the print was still wet, Brains began examining it with his powerful magnifying glass. I didn't savvy what he hoped to gain and I said so.

"Well," Brains said, "our cause might be helped considerably if I could learn the identity of the person who pasted up this message and sent it."

"How in the dickens can you hope to do that?" I said. "Handwriting or typing might be traced, sure. But a paste-up job like this seems to me to be a dead end."

"Not necessarily," Brains said. "When I examined the original I became quite convinced that the letters had been clipped mainly, if not entirely, from magazine covers. Not only that, from the very titles of the magazines."

"So what?" I said.

"The title or name of each magazine is quite distinctive," Brains went on. "For instance, the name, *National Geographic Magazine*, is done in a certain style. So is the title of the *Saturday Evening Post* and *Life* and the rest of them. These styles are often so distinctive that by seeing just a part of a title or even one letter, it is entirely possible to identify the name of the magazine the portion came from."

Brains picked up a metal letter opener and leaned over the photograph.

"For instance," he said, "I feel quite satisfied that this pasted 'R' in the message and this small 'd' and this large 'D' were cut from a *Reader's Digest* title. And I'd bet that this 'S' and 'L' and 'T' came from a *Sports Illustrated* cover."

Brains hunched closer and his voice got a little shriller. "See this 'E' and the 'M' and 'I' and this 'T'—typical of the letters used in the title of *Time*."

I could see what he was driving at O.K. Yet for the life of me I couldn't figure out what good it would do. Brains guessed I was still up a tree.

"You're thinking, of course, that thousands upon thousands of people have those magazines I mentioned," he said. "So how could there be a hope of finding the person who put this message together. Of course, you are right. Yet, there is a hope because some letters pasted on the message are completely unfamiliar to me."

"You mean those really slanty ones?" I asked.

"Excellent observation, Jimmy," Brains said. "Yes, those letters interest me extremely. I would like to learn the name of the magazine they were clipped from."

"But, gosh," I said, "even if you did find the name, what would that prove?"

Brains leaned back in his chair. "If it turned out to be a technical magazine, it would tell us that our mystery man was likely interested in airplanes, or big-game hunting, or gardening or what not. And if this interest was odd or quite specialized it might enable us to finally trace the person we seek."

"Brother!" I said. "What a shot in the dark!"

"The smallest detail cannot be ignored, Jimmy," Brains said blandly.

I took a look at the lab clock and gulped.

"One detail I overlooked is I'll be late for supper unless I blast off," I said.

"On your way then," Brains said. "I'll see you in the tent at seven o'clock."

I was dog tired. And there was a TV western I wanted to see.

"How about a night off, X?" I said.

Brains' eyes zeroed in on me. "Very well," he said, quietly. "I'll contact Stony Rhodes."

"See you at seven," I said, and I hurried out of the lab before I was tempted to choke him.

That night at supper Mom and Dad did some yakking about the strange letter that was reported in the *Ledger*. My father seemed convinced that a crank had sent it and that it wouldn't help Will Parslow one bit.

I was anxious to find out all the dope I could on the old Gault place. But it wasn't until we were having dessert that I was able to quiz my dad.

"The Gaults?" he said. "Well, there was Jacob and his wife, and Jacob's brother, Nathan. They were a queer lot. One morning a peddler stopped by the house and found the door wide open. Jacob and his wife had been murdered. With a hatchet, I think. Not a trace of old Nathan Gault has ever been found. He just disappeared as if the ground had opened and swallowed him up."

I shivered. I wondered if it wouldn't be a good idea to let Stony take my place in the agency after all.

"The Gault farm went to seed. Soil there is no good now. I don't think you could raise a cactus on it." Dad gave me that narrowed look. "Why are you so interested?"

"Oh, nothing," I said. "Can I have more berries, Mom?"

It was a little before seven when I said to my folks, "Well, guess I'll be going. See you in the morning."

I found out quickly it wasn't that simple. When I pushed my bike out of the garage, my dad called to me from the porch.

"Do you need that to go a couple of blocks, Jimmy? Pretty soon you'll forget you have legs."

"Maybe Brains will want to take a ride around town before it gets dark," I said.

"Better leave it here," my dad said.

I started to give him an argument, then shut up. You had to get up awful early in the morning to pull the wool over his eyes.

"Okay, okay," I said.

I wondered how Brains was going to like carrying me on his handlebars. What was I getting sore about? I didn't want to go out to that spooky place tonight anyway. I grinned at Dad just as he turned around and went back into the house.

When I got to the tent Brains was not there, but Stony Rhodes was.

"What are you doing here?" I asked.

"It's a free country, isn't it?" he asked.

"Yeah," I said. I'm great at snappy comebacks.

Brains was always on time. I was sure he'd been there. Then I saw the mirror that was placed against the flashlight on an old grocery carton next to Brains' cot. About a week before, Brains had said he hated leaving written messages around.

I sat down on the cot and idly picked up the mirror.

"Hey, Stony," I said, "do I hear Brains coming?"

When Stony went to the front of the tent and looked out, I breathed on the mirror. The message had been written on it with French chalk. Then Brains had rubbed it off with a cloth. The message became visible again when you breathed on it. It said, I'M AT THE LAB. B.

"I don't see him," Stony said.

"I guess he won't be here for a couple of hours," I said, and stretched out. "Think I'll take a snooze."

Stony hung around for a while, then left. I made sure he was gone before I hurried over to the lab. The sky was clouding up overhead and I thought I heard a rumble of thunder far off.

Brains barely looked up from the book he was reading when I came in. I told him about Stony making me late and about my dad putting thumbs down on the bicycle.

Finally he shut the book and said, "This book I got from the library yesterday explains the geological structure of our state, particularly in this area. No such soil as you see in that jar occurs anywhere in the state. I am certain it is loam mixed with decayed vegetable matter."

"Sure," I said, "but listen, did you hear about my not having a bicycle?"

"It does not matter," Brains said. "Shortly after you left for supper I took a walk downtown to get the newspaper. I met Ben Carlin in Bennett's Drugstore. You'd say he was to be trusted, wouldn't you?"

"Far enough, I guess."

"I told Ben about our hearing the strange sounds out by the Gault place and asked him would he mind driving us out there tonight." Brains rubbed his palms together and turned loose that smug smile of his. "You see, if we hear them again, Operative Three, we will have someone to back us up if we should decide to tell the police."

"Not bad," I admitted.

"In case of a storm we can get under cover quick, too," Brains said.

At eight-thirty we were waiting for Ben at the corner of Maple and Capital. We heard him coming when he was still two blocks away. The car he'd got to replace his old green one sounded like a concrete mixer gone crazy. When he pulled to a stop his brakes shrieked and it wouldn't have surprised me any if the whole thing had fallen apart at the curb.

"What are you two detectives up to now?" Ben asked, and grinned. "You don't think there's a connection between that robbery and the old Gault place and that store dummy, do you? Ha!"

"Laugh if it makes you feel better," Brains said.

He spoke so quietly Ben didn't hear him. But I did.

It was sure dark when we got out of Ben's old sedan, about fifty yards down the road from the Gault place. We walked kind of slow the rest of the way. When we climbed up the high bank and got to the edge of the cellar, there was hardly a sound. Even the crickets had clammed up.

"I don't hear anything at all," Ben whispered. "I guess if you stayed here long enough you'd imagine you saw or heard anything."

"The sound we heard was no product of our imagination," Brains said.

Lightning flashed far off. It was followed by a roll of thunder.

"There's a little family cemetery over there," Ben said, pointing. "It's where all the Gaults are buried. Maybe their ghosts walk. Want to look at it, or are you scared?"

"Lead the way," Brains said stubbornly.

Being a member of the firm, I had to go along. A vice-president can't afford to chicken out.

The field we crossed was knee-high in coarse grass and weeds. It ended at a thick woods.

"It's right over on the other side of that stone wall," Ben said, "at the edge of the woods."

We had to watch our step getting over the wall. Some of it was covered with moss and was slippery as grease.

The next flash of lightning that came wasn't too bright but it lit up the old burying ground for a few seconds. The ancient gravestones were leaning every which way. There were about six of them in a tangle of brier bushes.

Then I saw it—a dark shadow against the trees not twenty feet away. It moved. I tried to yell but couldn't. I grabbed at Ben Carlin's arm and pointed.

"L—Look," I finally choked out.

There was another lightning flash. Brains gasped as if something had hit him in the stomach. A man in a long, dark coat stared at us and his eyes seemed to shine like rhinestones. His slouch hat was pulled low over his ears, and his collar was turned up. He had a beard.

"What are you doing here?" a deep, raspy voice said. "Who are you?"

We turned and ran. That is, Ben and I did. Brains slipped and fell. He called to us for help. I never was more scared in my whole life and I knew Ben was, too. Just the same, we stopped running and went back. The bearded man had grabbed Brains. I picked up a piece of an old tree limb and charged at him. He let go, then turned and raced off into the woods.

When Brains had found his voice and his glasses, he told us the man had put his fingers right around his throat and had shaken him like a rat. I noticed Brains kept his right fist clenched as we half walked and half ran back to the car.

I was sweating ice water. My legs felt like about as strong as strings of cooked spaghetti. Brains wasn't whistling or humming *The Farmer in the Dell*, I noticed.

Ben Carlin said, "Get in the car! Quick! Let's get out of here."

Nobody spoke a word for three miles. Then I swallowed what was left of the lump in my throat and said, "It must have been old Gault. We would pick the night when he decided to come back."

"Say, you could be right about it being old Gault," Ben said. "You sure were lucky he didn't cut your throat, Brains. Did he have a knife?"

"No," Brains said. "But his fingers were lethal enough. . . . I want to thank you both for coming to my rescue."

"Are you going to tell the police?" Ben asked him.

"Decidedly yes," Brains said.

Ben dropped us off in front of the Benton house. When we got into the tent in the back yard Brains plunked himself down on his cot and took a few deep breaths. "Get the flashlight, Jimmy," he said.

A few seconds later I was staring at something Brains held in the palm of his hand. It was a small black button.

"I pulled at my attacker's sleeve when he got his fingers around my neck. This came off," Brains said. "Ah! There's an anchor on it which seems to indicate that he wore a sailor's coat."

9 SECRET MISSION

About seven-thirty the next morning I went home to get washed up and have breakfast. And with every step I tried to think of a way to tell my folks about what had happened out at the old Gault place. I mean, I wanted to tell them in such a way that would make them think I hadn't planned to go there. But I couldn't figure anything out and it began to look as if I'd have to come out with the hard truth.

As I took my place at the table, Mom gave me the once-over. "Your eyes are a little puffed, Jimmy," she said. "You look kind of pale under that tan. I don't believe you sleep well in that tent."

"You are a little green around the gills," Dad said.

I took a deep breath. "Well," I said, "Last night . . ."

Talk about being saved by the bell. Right then the front doorbell sounded!

My mother went to answer it. When she came back—ye gods and little fishes—she had Chief Hadley with her. And right back of the Chief was—Brains!

77

I guessed then that Ben Carlin had gone to the police station after he had let us out the night before.

My father looked at the Chief, at Brains, then at me. He shoved his chair back.

"What did they do this time, Chief?" he asked.

Chief Hadley took his time about answering. He cleared his throat, put on a stern expression and said, "Something happened last night, Mr. and Mrs. Carson, which you must be informed about. Ben Carlin told me that he picked up your son and Barclay Benton last night to take them for a short ride. As they went past the old Gault place, they got curious and took a look around. . . ."

Then the Chief came out with the whole story as Ben had given it to him.

"Great Heavens!" Mom said. "Barclay, you might have been killed!"

Then she went pale and looked at me. "And you, too!" It's so nice to know you'd be missed.

"Has the man been caught yet?" Dad asked.

Chief Hadley shook his head. "We're scouring that whole area, Mr. Carson. Sent out an all-points broadcast. If the fellow is within fifty miles of here we'll have him before nightfall. I stopped by so I could get the details from your boy, too. Wanted the stories to jibe, of course."

"It's just the way you heard it from Ben," I said, "only he didn't pull a knife."

Brains nodded.

"Young Benton here got a button off the man's coat in the struggle," Chief Hadley said. "It's from one of those dark raincoats navy men or merchant seamen wear."

"You think it could be Nathan Gault?" my father asked.

"It's possible," Chief Hadley said. "Good way for a man to disappear for a long time is to go to sea. Anyway, after all these years I don't think they can try him for murder. Never was any proof he did it."

"No more proof, I'll wager, than you've got against Will Parslow," Brains said.

The Chief chose to ignore my partner's remark. But I knew it'd made him sore as a boil. He tipped his hat to Mom and left right after that.

My father took a big gulp of coffee. Then he shook his head. "If you two kids aren't separated, this town will have to call out the National Guard. Maybe you should break up this partnership!"

"I'm sorry you feel that way, sir," Brains said. "The Benton & Carson International Detective Agency is only trying to be of public service, to see that a man can walk the streets of this town with his head high and . . ."

The front doorbell rang again. This time it was Brains' father, Professor Benton. He was tall, almost as thin as his son and a little bit stooped. He was maybe ten years older than my dad.

"I was downtown getting fuel for my car when Chief Hadley picked up my boy, Mr. Carson," he said. "I thought I'd better come here and determine what is what, so to speak."

"Mr. Carson thinks I'm a bad influence on Jimmy, it would seem," Brains said.

Professor Benton said, "Well now!"

And my father said, "It's not that at all, Professor. I just think it's a crazy idea for two kids their age to do man-sized detective work."

"Size does not always count, Mr. Carson," Professor Benton said. He cleared his throat and tugged at the lapels of his coat. "Shall we have no little lyrics because Homer and Dante have written epics?"

"Huh?" my dad said.

"Perhaps because we have heard the great organ at Freiburg," Professor Benton went on, "the sound of a peasant girl's zither in an Alpine hut pleases us no more?"

My father just stared at the professor. Now if Brains' father had asked Pop who ran the wrong way for a touchdown in a Rose Bowl game he wouldn't have had to think for a minute. Right then, though, my father was way out in left field.

He cleared his throat a little nervously. "I . . . I think I get your point, Professor," he said.

"To put it more simply," Professor Benton said, "don't underestimate gifts that come in small packages. I am sure we can't judge our boys' activities the past few days as escapades, Mr. Carson. However, I do not presume to tell you how to bring up your son. As for myself, I believe in encouraging initiative. Barclay, here, is—now where did he go?"

Brains came out of the kitchen then, eating a big sugar doughnut.

Dad laughed. "I know what he is, Professor. He's just like any other kid." He looked at me. "It's all right, son. Just watch your step."

"See you in about an hour," Brains said. He walked up to my dad and stuck out his hand. "Thanks, Mr. Carson. I don't know what I'd do without Jimmy."

I could have told him. He'd have to do more than just sit in that chair in the lab and think, and give orders. He'd get the knees of his dungarees busted out and his shirts torn doing his own leg work. Or get strangled or something if I wasn't around.

When Brains and his father left, Dad said, "Whew-w-w!" and shook his head. "I feel like the village idiot."

"They *are* pretty smart," I said.

Dad looked me in the eye. "Don't think I'm going to give you too much rope, Jimmy. I'm setting a curfew for you, understand? You're to be in bed at ten-thirty every night. And don't think I won't check."

"Sure, okay," I said.

The *Daily Ledger* had the story on the front page of its noon edition. Brains and I read it in the crime lab. The headlines said: MYSTERIOUS ATTACK ON JUNIOR SLEUTHS. *Was It Nathan Gault? Did A Murderer Return To The Scene Of His Crime?*

"But for the heroic efforts of Benjamin Carlin and Jimmy Carson," the story said, "Barclay Benton, son of Professor Benton of Crestwood College, might not be alive today. After a terrible struggle, the assailant fled into the darkness of the woods . . ."

"Ben sure heaped it on when he told that story to Lew Jarman," I said to Brains.

"It is slightly exaggerated," Brains said. "Listen to this. . . . 'All the law enforcement agencies are scouring the area. State troopers are also on the alert.' "

Brains was about to toss the paper aside when suddenly he spotted another item on the front page and did a double-take.

"Jimmy! Look at this," he said.

I did. There under a smaller banner headline I read:
PARSLOW TRIAL SET FOR SEPT. 30th.

It went on to say that the County Prosecutor had filed a "criminal information" against Will Parslow. Exactly what that meant, I wasn't certain. But one thing I knew for sure—good-natured, kindly Will Parslow was going on trial for grand larceny!

"The trial's a week from next Thursday," said Brains. "They seem to be in an awful hurry to convict poor Will."

"Well, folks are pretty sore," I reminded him. "Remember, the five thousand dollars that were stolen belonged to the Community Camp Fund. The women in Crestwood worked for months to raise that money so there'd be a summer camp for the kids in town. Now that plan hasn't got the chance of a snowball on a hot griddle. So it stands to reason that they want the thief sent to prison."

"But Will Parslow isn't the thief. He *couldn't* be. Anyone who knows him could tell you that," said Brains indignantly.

"But that old prune-face, Mrs. Pruett, swears she saw Will in Harvey Beal's office the night the money was stolen," I said. "A jury might believe her, especially since Will hasn't got an airtight alibi for his whereabouts on the night in question."

"But the Widow Pruett's testimony is the only evidence against Will. If we could prove she was wrong—" Brains looked off into space and then suddenly I could see that Sherlock Holmes squint in his eyes.

"Jimmy," he snapped, "I've got an idea!"

"I'm listening," I said.

"Let's hope that store dummy is still out there by Boiling Pond," Brains said. "I'm sure you can ride it into town on your handlebars."

"*Me?*" I said. "I'd sure look stupid doing a thing like that. What do we want that dummy for?"

"I'll explain later," Brains said.

"I'd hoped I'd seen the last of that thing," I said. "All right, let's go."

"Not now," Brains said. "We have to bring it in after dark. First we must pay a visit to Mr. Beal."

So we called at Mr. Beal's office after lunch and when I heard what was in Brains' mind it didn't sound so crazy after all. Mr. Beal leaned back in his chair and chuckled when Brains got through talking.

"You're a pretty smart kid, Benton," he said. "Sure hope it works. Around nine-thirty? I'll be here to let you in."

Suddenly Mr. Beal raised a finger. "Just a moment, son. Your plan depends on the presence of Police Chief Hadley. How do we know he'll be at the station when we need him."

"Elementary, Mr. Beal," said Brains patiently. "As a student of criminology I once undertook to study the daily life of a Chief of Police. And since Chief Hadley was the subject of my investigation I am thoroughly acquainted with his habits."

Listening to Brains talking in that superior way of his was nothing new to me. But poor Mr. Beal just stood there with his mouth wide open, like a fish out of water.

"At about eight-thirty every night the Chief leaves his house and returns to the police station," Brains continued. "There he plays checkers with the desk sergeant until about ten-thirty, at which time he returns home."

"My word!" said Mr. Beal. "I'd no idea the Chief was so devoted to duty!"

Brains smiled his most superior smile. "I suggest there may be another motive for Chief Hadley's behavior. You see he thoroughly enjoys the importance of his position and coming back to the station after supper gives him an extra few hours of ordering people around."

"I'm beginning to see the light," said Mr. Beal. "I'd sure hate to have you on *my* trail, son."

I could swear Brains grew at least six inches taller under Mr. Beal's admiring glance. But he tried hard to show that praise was beneath his notice.

"Come, Operative Three," he said. "We have important work to do." As we left the office Mr. Beal was still shaking his head in disbelief.

That afternoon Brains went to the public library to inspect its file of magazines. He took the photo of the pasted-up mystery note with him. When he returned he reported he'd found no magazines with letters in the title to match the unidentified ones in the note.

We stayed in the crime lab most of the afternoon with the short wave radio turned on. Reports kept coming in about the search for Nathan Gault, or whoever the mysterious assailant was. The police hadn't found a trace.

"How old did the *Ledger* say Gault was, or would be now?" Brains asked.

He pushed a button in the wall and a cot unfolded from a hidden closet and settled to the floor. Brains stretched out on it, his hands clasped over the back of his head.

I picked up the copy of the *Ledger* again and looked for Gault's description. "It says here he'd be over seventy now."

"You know something, Operative Three?" Brains said. "They will never find him."

"Wha-a-a-t?"

"I don't believe that was Gault. The hands of a man that age have knobby knuckles. The skin is wrinkled and the veins stick out."

"So?" I said.

"The hands that went around my neck didn't have knobby knuckles," Brains said decisively. "I felt them. They weren't old hands!"

Brains sat up abruptly, "That attack was another attempt to scare us off. When the noises failed, they tried something else!"

"Then," I said weakly, "you . . . you think there is something hidden out there?"

"Yes!" Brains said. "But I wish I knew what."

10 THE WITNESS

It was just getting dark when we parked our bikes and walked down the woods road leading to Boiling Pond. As we reached the edge of the clearing, Brains stopped and put his hand on my arm. It scared me.

"You hear something?" I whispered.

"No. Just stay still," Brains said.

All I could hear was the noise of millions of insects, and the croaking of frogs from where the little stream wandered away from the pond.

"It's all right, Operative Three," Brains said, finally. "As long as those frogs make a noise over there, there's nobody anywhere near the swamp."

Just the same, we were cautious as we made our way to where we hoped the dummy still was. I kept as far away from the edges of the pond as I could without climbing trees. Nobody was ever always a hundred per cent right, even Brains. If anybody was going to push me into that water he'd have to have mighty long arms.

We found the store dummy. We took turns carrying it over our shoulders back to where we'd left our bikes. Then, after a brief rest, I held my bike up while Brains tied the dummy to my handlebars. It was a spooky-looking thing, sitting there. Brains bent the legs and tied the feet to the metal arms on each side of the front wheel.

"Anybody seeing you will swear you've got a real passenger," Brains said.

"I hope this stunt works," I said, as I pushed the bike out onto the road.

We coasted down a long hill. The dummy tipped back against me and I almost fell off. At the foot of the hill we had to stop and fix it in place again. One of its arms hung by a piece of wire, and when I started pedaling again that arm kept striking against the bike frame and going clank-clank-clank! It gave me the willies.

We rode into Crestwood well after dark, by way of Sugden's lumberyard. There were only a few houses in that part of town. Going down Spruce Street we saw the headlights of a car up ahead and I steered quickly into a side street. When the car passed, we didn't lose any time getting to the narrow street in back of the building where Mr. Beal had his office. Nobody had seen us. So far, so good.

"It's nine-thirty," Brains whispered as we cut the dummy loose from my bike. "The Widow Pruett closes her store at ten."

"Right," I said.

We carried the dummy around to the front and up the flight of stairs to Mr. Beal's office. Brains rapped on the door. There was only a thin crack of light showing under it.

Mr. Beal swung the door open and we hurried inside.

"Anybody see you?" Mr. Beal asked.

Brains shook his head. "You got those old clothes, Mr. Beal?"

"Right there on the table, Barclay."

We dressed the dummy up in a shirt and a tie, and an old blue serge coat. Brains put it in a chair behind the desk.

"H-m-m," Mr. Beal chuckled, "he looks more intelligent than a lot of the fellows who have worked for me."

Brains made sure the stage was set right. Only one light was burning, over the desk, and the shade was raised at the window that looked right across at the one in Widow Pruett's living quarters above her stationery store.

"Be sure to keep out of sight," Brains told Mr. Beal. "You, too, Jimmy."

Brains scootched down behind the chair holding the dummy. Then we waited.

A little after ten o'clock, the lights went on in the widow's apartment. She puttered around for a while, then made herself a cup of tea. She came over to the window and put the cup on a small table. Then she finally plunked down in her chair and reached for her knitting.

Five minutes went by. The widow took a sip of tea, settled back again. Then she lifted her eyes and stared right into Mr. Beal's office. Brains pushed the dummy forward a little, then moved the arms. The widow kept looking.

Brains said under his breath, "If she turns her head away or gets up to get something, Jimmy, I'll turn out that light. You pull down the shade right after."

"Supposing this doesn't work," Mr. Beal said from where he was squeezed behind a filing cabinet.

"I believe it will be successful," Brains said. "Look at her when she knits. Her nose is right against the needles."

We waited for almost fifteen minutes before the Widow Pruett got up from her chair. It looked like she was going to pour herself another cup of tea. Brains didn't lose any time putting out the light and I jumped across the room and yanked the shade down.

"You're through working for the day, Mr. Beal," Brains said. He grinned.

"What do we do with that thing now?" asked the real Mr. Beal.

"You mean the witness for the defense?" Brains said. "He's going right down to the police station with us. I want him to tell Chief Hadley whatever he knows."

Chief Hadley! The thought of facing him again made me wince. He'd warned us to stay out of his hair, and here we were meddling in the Parslow case again.

Did I say meddling? Creeps! We were in it up to our ears!

It was just as Brains had predicted. We found Chief Hadley smack in the middle of a red-hot game of checkers. His opponent was Sergeant Hawkins. You could tell the Chief was winning. The toothy grin on his full-moon face was like a neon sign.

But that grin sure turned sour when we walked in dragging that dressed-up dummy.

He was sputtering like the fuse on a firecracker when Mr. Beal said, "Oh, Chief Hadley! Could we speak to you privately for a moment?"

Hadley frowned for a minute. "All right," he said. "In here!" He led us into his office and closed the door.

"All right," he said. "Now what's this all about. What are you doing here with that dummy? If this is some kind of shenannigan—"

"Now, Chief," said Mr. Beal soothingly. "The boys have some important information. Better hear them out."

But Hadley wasn't letting anyone smooth his feathers—not just yet. We were in his bailiwick and he was out to show us he was the head rooster in this back-yard.

"Look here, Harvey," he growled. "It's bad enough having these two little hawkshaws butting into police affairs without you getting in on it too. If you think I'm going to let you clutter up this police station with that piece of junk—"

That was when Brains interrupted him. "That piece of junk happens to be a star witness in the Parslow case," he said.

"The star witness? Just what kind of a gag is this?" shouted Hadley.

"As I said before," Beal cut in, "you'd better hear these boys out." And there was something in the quiet way he said it that made the chief stop bellowing and start listening.

"All right," he said, "let's have it."

Brains let him have it. In a few well-chosen words he explained his idea and the purpose of the dressed-up dummy.

"If our plan works we could prove once and for all whether or not Mrs. Pruett really saw Will Parslow in Mr. Beal's office the night the money was stolen."

Yes, as a plan it was a dandy—a real smart piece of detective work. There was just one thing wrong. Chief Hadley wasn't buying it.

"If you think I'm going to take part in this crazy scheme you're all out of your minds," he snapped. "I'm not going to drag Mrs. Pruett down here in the dead of night just to question her. If that gossipy old biddy ever got sore at me she'd talk me right out of my job with all those poison rumors she spreads."

"It could mean your job if you *don't* cooperate with us," said Mr. Beal. "If the boys are right and you're wrong it'll all come out at the trial. And believe me, the citizens of Crestwood won't think much of a police chief who was outsmarted by a couple of amateurs, and kids at that."

Kids! Amateurs! Brains and I looked at each other indignantly. It looked like folks would never learn that we were professional investigators—and the best in the business to boot!

But a second later we forgot about being sore, because it looked like Mr. Beal's plain talk was just what the doctor ordered. Chief Hadley got the message.

"Well, okay. You fellows may have made a lucky guess at that," he grumbled. "All right. I'll go along with the plan. But if I get in any kind of a jam I'll remember just who started the whole thing."

And the way he looked at Brains and me, I could almost hear those cell doors clanging shut.

Hadley opened his office door and bellowed down the hall. "Hey, Hawkins! Head down to the Widow Pruett's house and bring her back here. I've got a few questions I want to ask her."

"Bring her back *here*? But it's after ten, Chief. She'll be mad as a singed cat! Can't it wait till morning?"

"I want her here *now!*" roared Hadley. The sound of it nearly lifted the roof off the police station. It was obvious that the Chief wasn't used to having his orders questioned.

Except maybe by Benton and Carson.

Anyway, Hawkins shot out of there like a guided missile. But as we heard the outer door slam shut behind him, the Chief let go with another bellow.

"*Hey!* Where are you going with that thing?"

I spun around. Brains was dragging the dummy through a side door into another room.

"Pray calm yourself, Chief Hadley," said Brains soothingly, as if he were talking to a fretful child. "I am merely moving the dummy out of sight. We don't want it around till the critical moment comes."

"Oh! Oh, yeah!" said the Chief, flushing. "I was just about to suggest it myself."

In a pig's eye, he was!

"And you'd better step inside this other room, too, Mr. Beal," Brains added.

"I understand," said Beal. "We don't want to put Mrs. Pruett on her guard." He stepped through the door.

Funny! There was Brains—nothing more than a walking,

carrot-topped beanpole of a schoolboy. But when he talked in that commanding tone of his, even older folks listened. And took orders, too.

Anyway, both Mr. Beal and the dummy were both out of sight when Mrs. Pruett charged in a few minutes later with Sergeant Hawkins right behind her. And, brother, was she mad!

Did I say mad? The sergeant had been right. She *did* sound like a singed cat.

"The impudence of it! To drag me down here like a common criminal!"

"Sergeant Hawkins, did you drag Mrs. Pruett?" asked Hadley.

Hawkins wiped his brow. "Believe me, Chief, if anyone was dragged it was *me*."

"Okay. You'd better get back to the desk now," said Hadley, closing the door behind Hawkins.

"And now perhaps you'll have the goodness to explain this outrage," fumed Mrs. Pruett.

"Now calm down, Mrs. Pruett. I just got some new information on the Parslow case and I wanted to ask you a few more questions."

"Well, I gave my testimony to the Prosecuting Attorney the other day. I don't see why I have to go through it all over again. If honest, decent folk are going to be hounded like this, then it's time that Crestwood got a new Chief of Police!"

Man, that hit Hadley right where he lived. "Now wait a minute, Mrs. Pruett, you've got me all wrong," said the Chief, pleadingly.

But old prune-face wasn't listening. She had the whip hand and she wasn't letting go.

"I'm leaving now," she said, heading for the door. "Just you wait until tomorrow. You'll find that Sarah Pruett is not without influence in this town."

Well, that was it. She had Hadley so buffaloed he was letting her go without asking her a single one of the questions we'd been planning on. If she went out that door our whole case went out the door with her.

11   THE TRAP

Then brains went into action!

"Mrs. Pruett," he said, "if you leave this room without answering Chief Hadley's questions you will be guilty of obstructing justice."

Mrs. Pruett had her hand on the doorknob when she heard Brain's squeaky voice behind her. Now she whirled around with her mouth wide open like a fly-trap.

You see, Brains and I had been sitting on a low leather couch in a corner of the Chief's office where the light wasn't very good. It was obvious that old prune-face hadn't seen us until Brains spoke up.

But now that she had us in her sights her mouth pursed up as if she'd just bitten into a lemon.

"And just what are these two doing here, Chief Hadley?"

He gulped. "They're the ones that brought in the new information on the Parslow case. That's why we brought you here to ask a few more questions."

"Which I suggest you answer, Mrs. Pruett," said Brains, importantly. "Remember! In this state, conspiracy to obstruct justice is punishable with a prison term of from one to five years."

When he speaks in his official voice, Brains sounds like a judge or governor. But at that moment he sounded like the voice of doom itself.

And it worked. Sarah Pruett turned white as a sheet.

"Well, all right," she said, her voice cracked and trembling. "I'll answer the questions if it's so important. After all, I am an honest, law-abiding citizen."

"Very well then, we will proceed," said Brains.

"Now, just a minute! I'll do all the questioning around here," interrupted Hadley angrily. Now that Brains had softened her up, suddenly Hadley was ready to take over. Wouldn't you know it?

"Let's start with the night of the robbery. Are you sure you saw Will Parslow in Mr. Beal's office that night?"

Her face tightened up confidently. Sarah Pruett was on familiar ground now. "Just as I told the Prosecutor," the widow said. "I saw him as plain as all get out. Oh, at first I didn't want to believe it. Told myself I was seeing things. But when I heard the place was robbed, it came back as plain as day. Yes! I saw Will Parslow that night!"

"By the way, what were you doing at your window, Mrs. Pruett?" Hadley was asking the question exactly the way Brains had suggested.

"Why I was knitting, as you know very well. I always knit whenever I have a free moment. Everyone knows that."

"Yes, I've seen you myself many times. But you hold those needles mighty close to your eyes. Don't you think you ought to get yourself a pair of strong glasses?"

Hadley spoke in a neighborly kind of voice, like a good friend. But Sarah Pruett was nobody's fool. She saw the trap he had baited for her.

"Chief Hadley, I can knit with my eyes shut," she snapped. "And I can see as well as the next person when I have to."

"Then you're certain it was Will Parslow you saw the night of the robbery, and not someone else—say, Mr. Beal?"

"It was Will I saw and none other," she said grimly. And the cold cruel way she said it told you that if there was anyone in this world she hated it was Will Parslow. And she'd never forgive him making her pay the doctor bills when he slipped and broke his leg on her icy walk.

"Now then," said Hadley, "you'd know Mr. Beal if you saw him at his office window? Let's say Mr. Beal was working at his desk tonight. Would you recognize him if you saw him at his desk?"

"As a matter of fact I did see him tonight," said the widow triumphantly. "Just as plain as you sitting there at your own desk, Chief Hadley!"

From his desk Hadley gave us a sharp commanding look. "All right, you two, bring on your witness."

In an instant we dragged the dummy in from the next door.

"What in the world is going on here," asked the widow, puzzled. There was a squeaky frightened note in her voice, like a rodent that suspects a trap.

"This is the gentleman Mrs. Pruett saw tonight in Mr. Beal's office, Chief," said Brains.

The widow shot out of her chair as if it was on fire. "That's a lie!" she screeched. "You wretched little boy! You know it's a lie!"

She turned to the Chief. "I tell you it was Mr. Beal I saw in his office tonight. If he was here he'd tell you himself!"

"I *am* here!" It was Mr. Beal that spoke as he came in through the side door. "It was the mannequin you saw at my desk. I helped arrange the whole thing. You see, we were checking to find out if your eyesight was good enough to identify the man who stole the Camp Fund money from my office."

"Sarah Pruett, you're a mean-tongued, gossipy old crow," said Hadley. He was having his innings, now, and he was enjoying it. "Anyone who would lie a man like Will Parslow into the penitentiary—"

The widow had been sitting there stunned, but now suddenly she was herself again.

"The nerve of you, tricking me like that! A fine thing when the Chief of Police is allowed to browbeat a woman like this. Well, I'll have you know I'm a State's Witness against Will Parslow. And I'm not going to change my testimony at the trial no matter how many tricks you pull!"

She hissed the words like a snake as she went through the door.

"Well," said Brains, when she had gone, "I guess that washes out the case against Will."

"It probably does," said Hadley pursing his lips. "I'd better call the Prosecuting Attorney and tell him what happened." He reached for the phone on his desk and began to dial.

"Well, boys, you've done your duty. But it's a lucky thing I was here to do the questioning or we'd never have trapped her. Anyway, you'd better leave everything in my hands."

Leave everything in his hands! Brother, it took us only a minute to find out why he wanted it that way.

You should have heard him tell the story to the prosecutor on the phone. He made it sound like trapping Mrs. Pruett was all his idea. Oh, sure, he mentioned Brains and me once or twice but even the way he did it made us sound like a couple of idiots who'd kept him from solving the case a week sooner.

Brains and I were pretty sore, but the thought that Will would be out of trouble now was all the payment we wanted . . .

But it developed that Will Parslow wasn't out of the woods yet. If Mrs. Pruett refused to change her testimony then it was better for Will to have the case come to trial. At least that way his name would be cleared out in the open, where everyone could see that old Prune-Face Pruett was lying.

So we left it at that. But before leaving the police station Chief Hadley warned us not to say anything to anyone about how we'd sprung the trap on the widow Pruett. We weren't to say anything even at the trial.

"Remember! If you want Will to go free you've got to let me handle everything. After all I'm experienced in courtroom procedure and I'll know just how to go about it. Of course the judge may want to call you to corroborate some of the minor details . . ."

"Of course . . ." said Brains.

"Why the big fraud!" exclaimed Mr. Beal as we walked down the street. "He wants to hog all the credit for himself."

"Pray do not distress yourself, Mr. Beal," said Brains. "The main thing is that Will Parslow will be cleared at the trial. After all, Chief Hadley did cooperate in our little scheme, so let him have some of the glory."

But keeping quiet about the case wasn't easy, let me tell you. In the days that followed, all Crestwood was buzzing about the trial. Of course everyone was sure that Mrs. Pruett's testimony would send Will to prison. He'd probably confess right there on the stand.

Hearing all that nonsense it was mighty hard to keep my tongue under control. And once or twice there were a couple of close calls. Like that time at breakfast, the day before the trial.

"It's an open and shut case," said my mother. "Sarah Pruett saw Will in Beal's office. Of course she doesn't like Will, but I don't think she'd lie about a thing like that."

"Oh, wouldn't she, though," I blurted. And then everybody looked at me as I pretended to be eating my cereal.

"Jimmy, you look like the cat that swallowed the canary," said my father. "Just what do you know about all this?"

I tell you I came mighty close to spilling the beans right then, but I shoved a spoonful of cereal into my face and muttered a few indistinct words. Mother said something about it being bad manners to talk with food in your mouth. By the time I finished swallowing the cereal everyone had forgotten the whole thing.

Well, the day of the trial came at last. I guess just about everybody and his grandmother tried to get into the courtroom. Brains and I were there over an hour before it started. We were sitting with Mr. Beal and Mr. Westrell, the lawyer who was going to defend Will Parslow. Mr. Westrell had only been out of Law School about two years and had just started practicing in Crestwood.

The crowd in the courthouse was buzzing with rumors and talk about Will's case. But the buzzing turned into a positive roar when the whole thing was over a short half-hour later.

Yes, that's all the time the trial took. Everything turned out even better than Brains and I had hoped for. Right after the judge whammed down his gavel to start the trial, the prosecutor got up to say that Mrs. Pruett, the principal witness, was changing her testimony. And that since she was the only one to place Will Parslow at the scene of the crime, the state had no case against the defendant.

Of course Mrs. Pruett's change of heart caught us by surprise, but later we found out what had happened. It seems that just before the trial the prosecutor had warned the old biddy that if it was proved that she was deliberately lying, she'd be guilty of perjury, as well as obstructing justice . . .

That was all she needed. Sarah Pruett withdrew her testimony. Of course the judge had to get the details about who had proven the witness to be in error. That's when Chief Hadley got up to reap the glory.

But that judge was no fool. He knew the chief from away back. And he knew Hadley couldn't rig up that test for the widow's eyesight. Not in a million years. After that it only took a few more questions before Brains and I were called to the stand.

Then the judge complimented us as two public-spirited young citizens that Crestwood should be proud of. After that, Mr. Westrell led the courtroom in applauding us.

I noticed one person who didn't applaud. It was Mrs. Pruett. She was pushing her way out of the courtroom with a poison mean look on her face.

The judge dismissed the case and banged his gavel for the last time. You should have seen the mob scene that followed.

Brains and I shook hands with Will Parslow and Mr. Westrell just as a flashbulb went off. Mr. Parslow could hardly talk, he was that grateful. We could still hear the widow out in the corridor, yakkity-yakking and threatening to get even with everybody.

We met Ben Carlin outside. Ben was grinning from ear to ear.

"You kids sure knocked over the apple cart," he said. "Did you ever!"

A lot of people stopped and shook hands with us. But a lot didn't. I heard one man call us a couple of smart alecks and if we belonged to him he'd sure whack the tar out of us. I think Chief Hadley felt that way, too, from the look he gave us.

We didn't feel like heroes as we headed for the crime lab. Like Brains said, we'd only proved that the Widow Pruett didn't have much better eyesight than a bat. Will Parslow was still under a cloud. And he would be until the guilty party was found.

Somebody came running up behind us. I was afraid to look around in case it was Stony Rhodes.

It was.

"Gee, you'll get your names in the paper again," Stony said. "Maybe you could get mine in, too. Huh, Barclay? How I help you sometimes, and—"

"I know how you can get your name in the paper easy," I said.

"How?" Stony was all eager beaver.

"Go over to the Widow Pruett's and throw a brick through her window."

"You think you're pretty funny, don't you, Jimmy Carson?" Stony said in his piping voice. "Well, someday I'll get square with you. Just wait and see!"

"I'll wait," I said. "I'll wait a long time. Glad to."

When I walked into the house at lunchtime, I got a surprise. My seventeen-year-old sister, Ann, was there. She'd spent the whole summer as a counsellor at a girls' camp upstate. Then, when the camp closed at the end of August, Ann had gone visiting friends at Lake Carmine until school started. She'd come home just to get some more clothes. How do you like that for a nutty reason?

"Well, it's the big wheel," my sister said. She grabbed me and kissed me on the cheek and I rubbed it off with my sleeve. "Up at the lake everybody wants your autograph. Mom, his head looks bigger than ever."

"Very funny," I said. Then I grinned. "Wait'll you hear the local broadcast at twelve o'clock."

Ten minutes later it came over. I kept on eating my lunch as if it was nothing. But I was all pins and needles.

"—And with that store dummy that caused so much excitement a few days ago, Barclay Benton and Jimmy Carson, both of Crestwood, completely discredited the prosecutor's star witness, Mrs. Sarah Pruett. Will Parslow, when released—"

"Good grief, Mom!" my sister said.

"I don't like any of it," Mom said. "Sometimes I wish the Bentons would move as far away as—er—Timbuktu."

I knew she didn't mean it.

12 HURRIED SEARCH

BRAINS AND I SPENT THE BEST PART OF THE AFTERNOON IN THE lab reviewing the various things that had happened since that day when we'd spotted the stolen car at the bottom of Boiling Pond. Most of the questions that had plagued us right along were still unanswered.

Why had Ben Carlin's car been ditched in Boiling Pond, instead of just being abandoned?

Why had the dummy been put in it?

Who had written that strange note informing the police that Will Parslow was innocent of the robbery?

Why was somebody trying to scare us away from the Gault place?

Who was the man who'd attacked Brains at the old cemetery?

Brains and I finally gave up trying to figure it all out.

"I sure flunked the course," I said. *"Creeps!"*

"I certainly didn't post any passing grade," Brains said. He frowned. "Perplexing and exasperating. Particularly the identity of the writer of that note. I must keep probing into that."

"How?" I asked.

Brains thumbed his glasses back on the bridge of his nose. "Tomorrow, I'm going to Middlebury to get a book for my father," he said. *The Canaanite Period of Syrian History.*

"Boy," I said. "I just can't wait to read that one."

Aside from a sharp glance in my direction, Brains chose to ignore my remark. "While in Middlebury, I intend to examine the extensive display of magazines at Keller's Drugstore. Perhaps I'll find one with a title to match those italic letters. . . . I'd like you to come along, Jimmy. But I don't know if your parents would approve. We have put them under quite a strain recently."

I knew what he meant. I'd a feeling that Pop was about ready to really clamp down on me.

"Well, I can ask," I said.

I did at supper time. It turned out to be a cinch. Mom thought it was a splendid idea for me to get out of Crestwood for a day to let the excitement wear off. And my father agreed.

"I just don't like all this publicity Jimmy and Barclay are getting," Mom said to my dad. "How do you think I'm going to feel at the Garden Club meeting Monday afternoon? I can just hear the whispering. 'That Benton boy and that Jimmy Carson!' And the looks I'll get. Like I'm a delinquent parent."

"They're just plain jealous that it's not their own kids," Dad said. "I can't see where the boys have done anything wrong. If and when they do, I'll be the first one to step on them."

My sister said, "Humph!" She got up from the table. "You always did let him get away with murder."

"If they had," I said, "you would've been missing long ago."

"Stop that!" Dad said, "or your trip to Middlebury is off."

I shut up extra fast.

The city of Middlebury was about forty miles directly north of Crestwood. It was a big place. A real center. The circus always came there and the Middlebury Fair was famous all over the state and the Middlebury Mustangs had won the regional football championship for the last five years. But maybe the thing the city was best known for was the annual Columbus Day Road Race.

They'd been having this race since 1910, or some prehistoric time. And they'd kept pretty much to the same rules. I mean, all you had to do was soup up a car to look and sound like a racer and you were in. Of course, you had to have a hundred bucks for the entry fee and the race committee had to inspect your machine to judge that it was safe. But there weren't any qualifying heats and stuff like that.

The race was held at the fairgrounds on the old harness racing track. Drivers came from all over the country. There were big money prizes and the race was covered on TV and radio. The winner usually cashed in on endorsing the tires he used and the gas and the oil and stuff.

I mention the road race here because when the bus that Brains and I were taking to Middlebury pulled into the Crestwood station at nine o'clock the next morning, the first thing I saw was a huge sign advertising the race. It was plastered along the entire side of the bus:

DON'T DARE MISS—

THE MIDDLEBURY COLUMBUS DAY ROAD RACE
Thrills! Excitement! Speed!

And inside the bus, there was a handbill at every seat, plugging the road race.

Brains read the handbill and grimaced.

"They are starting the publicity early this year," he said. "I scarcely see why. The event always draws an overflow crowd. Ridiculous when you think of it—people paying money to watch men drive round a track in a furious effort to get nowhere."

I wasn't going to tangle with Brains. I knew how he felt about things like this. He'd never been to the big race and I don't think you could get him there with a gun.

But plenty of other people in Crestwood were just the opposite. My dad, for instance. He rarely missed the race, and for the last couple of years he'd taken me along. But the real racing fan was Ben Carlin.

You'd think that his father having been killed in the race would've soured Ben. Not at all. Each year Ben had a trackside seat, and once it was rumored that he'd even worked in the pits. Of course nothing was said about this openly because of Ben's uncle, Sam Lufkin, who'd had to swear to Ben's dying mother that he'd keep the boy from even getting into a racing car.

Well, when Brains and I reached Middlebury, we were in for more posters and signs about the race. Whoever was in charge of publicity that year had really gone all out.

Brains knew exactly where to look for the book his father wanted. And, will you believe it, we found *The Canaanite Period of Syrian History* in the first place we tried. It was the only copy they had. And they'd had it for ten years. But, as the salesman pointed out, the book wasn't exactly on the best-seller list.

"Perhaps we'll be as fortunate in our own quest," Brains said to me, as we headed for Keller's.

Keller's Drugstore was in downtown Middlebury in the business section. It sold everything, even outboard motors. And the magazines—good gravy! The section extended half the length of the store.

Brains got out the photograph of the mystery note and we began checking the racks. Even though there were hundreds of magazines on display, the job didn't take very long. It was soon painfully clear that there just weren't any magazines in the store with a title done in slanting letters of the type used in the note.

Brains snapped his fingers impatiently. "Of all the foul luck," he said.

He went over to one of the clerks and asked for the store manager. I was left standing while Brains talked to an elderly man the clerk pointed out. In a short while, my partner was back.

"I asked the manager where we might find magazines of smaller circulation, technical journals and such," Brains said. "We're to try a couple of places on Water Street."

Water Street turned out to be in the old part of town with many second-hand book shops. We drew a blank at the first store. Sure, they had lots of magazines, but of the same kind sold at Keller's.

The next shop we tried was dark and dingy and very dusty. The little old man who ran it looked like a gnome. He just grunted when Brains asked him about magazines.

"Thousands," he said, jerking his thumb toward the rear of the shop.

We threaded our way down an aisle that was piled high on either side with second-hand books. At the rear we found a counter and it was stacked, no kidding, almost to the ceiling with magazines.

"These are all back numbers, Jimmy," Brains said, "but any recent issue of the magazine we're looking for should serve to . . ." Brains' voice trailed off.

Now, this may be hard to believe. But you'll have to take my word for it. After all, I was there. I saw Brains reach out. I saw him gingerly take hold of a magazine and pull it free. I noticed that it was of digest size. But that's all I noticed before Brains let loose a Tarzan yell.

"Jimmy! Look! This is it! This is it!"

He held up the magazine. The title was *Road Racing* and it was done in those slanty letters with the line slashing across them, as though the letters themselves were going about eighty miles an hour. I didn't have to check the photo to know that the letters in that name were in the same exact style as those used in the mystery note.

The copy of the magazine was over a year old and pretty beat up. Not that Brains cared. I'd rarely seen him so elated.

"Come on," he said to me.

He paid the little old gnome fifteen cents and we got out to the street.

"This is one of the greatest breaks we've had," Brains said to me.

"I honestly don't see how it gets us as far as first base," I said. "The person who sent that note had one of these magazines lying around. O.K. So maybe that makes him interested in car racing."

"Right," Brains said. "He's an automobile racing enthusiast or the chances are he wouldn't subscribe to a highly specialized magazine like this one."

"I go along with that," I said. "But listen, Crestwood is full of racing car bugs. So is Middlebury and points north, south, east and west. My dad's a nut on it. So is Ben Carlin. So is Lew Jarman. So's Mr. Beal. And so is heap-big Police Chief, Hadley. I could go on."

"Please don't," Brains said. "You have made yourself abundantly clear. Yet, you haven't dampened my enthusiasm, Jimmy. I believe this magazine is going to point a finger straight at the man who wrote that note."

"Well," I said, "I wish you luck."

All this time we were ambling along Middlebury's main drag. Brains looked at his wrist watch.

"The next bus for home leaves in half an hour," he said. "We have just time for some refreshments. This is on me, Jimmy. What will it be? A soda or a Cherry-Fizz, or both?"

Brains really was riding high. Lightning, they say, never hits in the same place twice. So I wasn't going to miss this opportunity.

"Both," I said.

13 DANGEROUS PLAN

After we returned to Crestwood we sort of marked time for the rest of the weekend. Brains had to go visiting relatives with his father and mother. And I went along for the ride when my folks drove Ann back to Lake Carmine on Sunday afternoon.

It was after dark when we headed for home. We had the car radio turned on and picked up the local newscast. It reported that the Crestwood police had about given up the search for the man who had attacked Brains out at the old cemetery. I couldn't understand where he'd gone to. A man doesn't evaporate into thin air.

Just before we arrived home, my mother remembered something. She remembered that when she was collecting for the Community Camp Fund, Mrs. Holzworth gave her a twenty-dollar bill that had been torn almost in half and then patched with Scotch tape.

"Great guns, Clara," my dad said. "You should've told the police about that long ago. They might have been able to trace the bill and get a line on the thief."

"I just didn't think of it," Mom said, worriedly. "I'll call Chief Hadley the first thing tomorrow."

My mother was making the phone call when I left for the crime lab the next morning. I found Brains working on an air-cooling system he was installing. He'd got hold of two large fans from a small factory outside town that had installed a modern system.

I told him about the mended twenty-dollar bill.

He didn't seem impressed.

"That bank note could have been spent days ago," Brains said. "And who'd remember it?"

"I just thought I'd mention it," I said. "You're the nut on not skipping trifling details. . . . I guess you heard that the police have given up looking for the guy who tried to strangle you."

"Yes, yes," Brains said, impatiently. "No wonder they couldn't apprehend him. He was wearing a disguise, I'm convinced."

Brains began dismantling one of the big fans.

"By the way, Operative Three," he said. "My father's taking that sample of dirt we found on Mr. Beal's stairway over to the college today. There are some summer students still there. He promised he'll have them analyze the sample in the chemical lab. We should get the result this afternoon."

"Good," I said. "Any other developments?"

"No," Brains said. Then, he lowered the wrench he'd been working with. "Well, I have put something into motion which may become a development, I suppose."

"What's that?" I asked, curiously.

Even though we were upstairs in the lab and the entire garage was guarded with a web of electronic burglar alarms, Brains dropped his voice to almost a whisper.

"I have taken another step in the search to ferret out the identity of the person who sent the mystery letter," he said.

"How?" I said.

He pointed with the wrench to a shelf where the copy of the magazine, *Road Racing*, was lying.

"On examining that magazine," he said, "I found that it was not published in the U.S., but in Canada."

"Does that prove anything?" I asked.

"No, but it indicates something quite important, I believe. You see, Jimmy, a technical magazine like this one appeals to just a limited group of readers. Not the general public. Therefore, it seems safe to say that its circulation must be quite small. Particularly in this country, it being a foreign publication. In fact, if you wanted to get *Road Racing*, I'm quite sure the only way to do so would be to send in a subscription to the magazine."

"Yeah," I said. "I guess that's right."

"So, yesterday I wrote to the editorial office of *Road Racing* in Toronto, Ontario, Canada," Brains said. "I enclosed three dollars and fifty cents for a year's subscription."

I stared at him. "I thought you hated car racing."

"I most certainly see little appeal in it," Brains said.

"Then why under the sun are you taking *Road Racing?*"

A funny light was in my partner's eyes. I could tell he was secretly pleased with what he'd done.

"Oh, I thought that if the editors got a subscription from me they might be more favorably disposed to answer my question."

"What question?" I said. This was getting deep.

"I simply inquired if they could tell me whether anybody else in Crestwood—or in the state, for that matter—also subscribed to their magazine. If so, I hoped they would send me the name as I'd very much like to meet him!"

"Brother!" I said. I was always flabbergasted by the way Brains' mind worked. "Do you think they'll tell you?"

"Yes," Brains said. "After all, there is a fraternal bond between people with a common interest—especially car racing enthusiasts. . . . Of course, I may have guessed wrong and there is no local subscriber. In that event, I'll have to work out some other way to learn the man's identity. Yet, I rather think we'll soon have an important piece to fit into the puzzle, Jimmy."

Brains turned back to his work. I just sat there looking, and feeling, as bright as a two-watt bulb. That Brains . . . no wonder he was president of the agency.

After a while I saw Brains pull open a drawer under his work-bench and start rummaging through it.

"Lose something?" I asked.

"No," Brains said. "Seems as if I'm out of friction tape. Maybe Ben Carlin has some he can spare."

"I'll go with you," I said. I needed fresh air, and then some.

We went over to the Acme Garage. Just as we were about to step inside we heard Ben's voice. He sounded as mad as a hornet. He was banging away at something with a hammer and we couldn't hear what he said. Then there was another voice. It wasn't full of sunshine either, and it was almost loud enough to reach out to the road.

"I'll come here any time I please!" it said.

Just as we walked in, Ben said, "Now look, you can push me just so far. I'll—" He looked up and saw us and changed expression quickly. "Hi, fellas. Been in any graveyards lately?"

The man with Ben snickered. "These the kid detectives you told me about?"

"Brains, Jimmy," Ben said, "this is Joe Keely, a friend of mine. Honest Joe they call him in Middlebury."

We shook hands with the man. He was about thirty-five years old and had a long face. His eyes were pale blue, the color of dungarees washed out too many times.

"Yeah, Honest Joe," Ben said. "Look out he don't sell you the city hall. Has a used car lot and sells auto parts on the side. What brings you here, Brains?"

"I need some friction tape," Brains said. "I thought you might spare me some."

"Sure thing," Ben said. "Over on the bench. Help yourself."

When we left, I said to Brains, "A friend of his? I'd hate to hear him talking to an enemy."

"Even friends get into arguments," Brains said.

I made sure I was at the Benton house around five that afternoon when Professor Benton arrived home. Brains and I waited until the professor had gone into his study, then we followed.

"Did you get the sample of dirt analyzed, Father?" Brains asked.

Professor Benton seemed startled at first and bewildered.

"Analyzed?" he muttered. Then, his expression cleared. He reached into his pocket and removed an envelope. "Yes, indeed. Quite interesting, too. Not much of the sample could be construed as ordinary soil. It was made up almost entirely of decayed vegetable matter, mostly the root variety, such as turnips, onions, and beets."

Brains stared at his father. He seemed stumped.

"What about those old dead seeds?" Brains asked.

Professor Benton pursed his lips and looked up at the ceiling. "H-h-m," he said after a while. "I can think of only one place where that sample you gave me might have come from, son. An old root cellar."

"A root cellar?" I asked him. "What's that?"

"Years ago, James," the professor said, "there were no frozen vegetables and farmers certainly couldn't keep a winter's supply of vegetables in an old-fashioned ice-box. So they dug a special cellar into a hillside or a high bank near their farms."

I could almost see Brains' ears prick up.

"Do you think there might have been a root cellar out at the old Gault farm?"

"Possibly," Professor Benton said. "In fact, probably."

When we got outside Brains said, "That old junk piled against the bank out at the Gault place, Jimmy! It could hide the front of an old root cellar."

"Now wait," I said, "I'm not going out there at night again!"

"Who said anything about night?" Brains asked. "I have more than one reason why it must be examined in the daylight."

I sighed with relief. I had two good reasons myself. One, I was scared of that old place in the darkness. Two, I wanted to catch a movie at the Cameo. It was about tracking down counterfeiters. I reminded Brains he'd said he wanted to see it, too.

"Very well," he said, "we'll make the early show around seven."

The movie turned out to be pretty good, although there could have been a little more action in it and more shooting. It was mostly scientific and that pleased Brains.

But by the time we got to the tent, he had forgotten that picture, I'm sure. He was all business and was making detailed plans for our expedition the next morning to the Gault place.

"If there *is* a root cellar out there," I said, uneasily. "Somebody could be hiding out in it."

"A distinct possibility," Brains said.

"Maybe it's Nathan Gault," I said. "Maybe we saw him, after all. The police naturally couldn't find him because he sneaked out only at night. He could have broken into Mr. Beal's office and swiped that camp money."

Brains shook his head. "It just doesn't add up that way, Jimmy," he said. He stretched and yawned. "We'd better turn in early tonight. We have a big day ahead of us. Perhaps a critical one. We'll need to have all our strength and all our wits about us."

It was a warm night, but I shivered.

14 OPERATION ROOT CELLAR

We were getting our bikes the next morning to begin Operation Root Cellar when Stony Rhodes came out of nowhere.

"Where you guys goin'?" he asked, his nose twitching like a chipmunk's, which he kind of looked like.

"We decided to join the Foreign Legion," I said. "Don't tell a soul."

"All right, wise guy," Stony said to me.

"We're just going to ride around, Stony," Brains said, mildly. He was a lot nicer to the pest than I ever could be.

"Swell," Stony said. "I've got my bike. I'll go with you."

You see how being nice to a character like that can trap you. But Brains rose to the occasion.

"Stony," he said, "maybe you could keep watch on Mr. Beal's office and make a note of everyone who goes in and out until we get back. Watch especially for a man wearing a dark beard and smoked glasses."

"Gee," Stony said. "A suspect?"

"Could be," Brains said.

I had to turn my back so that the little squirt couldn't see the grin on my face.

"I hate to trick him like that," Brains said as we rode away. "But I couldn't have him following us."

It took us about a half an hour to get to the old Gault place. In the bright sunshine there wasn't a thing about it that was scary, but we'd left our bikes nearly a half mile from the place and been mighty careful to sneak up without being seen. When we reached the heap of junk and stuff piled against the high bank, Brains knelt down in the sand. He picked up a handful and let it trickle through his fingers.

"It's easy to get rid of tracks in this fine sand, Jimmy. See that old broom there?"

He took some photographs from his pocket, studied them, then handed them to me. They were the ones he'd snapped a few days ago. He'd blown them up.

"Are these shots supposed to tell me something?" I asked.

"Look," he said, impatiently, and stabbed a finger at one of the photographs. "The broom was leaning against the wheel of the old hay-rake in this picture. But now it's resting against that coil of rusty barbed wire."

Darned if it wasn't.

"Some kids could've come by here, started fooling around and moved it," I said.

"Possibly," Brains admitted. "Yet, I'm going to assume they didn't."

Warning me not to touch anything, Brains stretched out full length in the sand and began working his way under the piled-up junk. Soon his head and shoulders were out of sight. I was afraid a lot of the old lumber and stuff would get dislodged and fall on him.

In a few minutes Brains put himself into reverse. On his feet again, he studied the situation a while. Then he attacked

from a different angle. This time he carefully removed two or three old boards, then tugged at what looked like a big piece of rusty sheet-iron. He made an opening in the pile of stuff big enough to slip through.

I got down on all fours and tried to follow him, but he called back, "Not enough room in here, Operative Three. You stay there and keep watch."

Brains backed out a little while later. Carefully, he replaced everything before he spoke. I knew from the expression on his face he'd found something.

"A root cellar, all right," Brains said. "It's got a pair of heavy wooden doors with a padlock on them half as big as your head."

"Couldn't you see through a crack or something?" I asked.

"Pitch dark inside. Even if there was a crack, there'd have to be a light inside to see anything."

"Maybe we could force the lock off," I said.

"Breaking and entering is a crime," Brains observed.

He was silent for a moment and I noticed that he was sniffing.

"I smelled something strong in there," he said. "Suggested an old oil rag. . . . Well, we'd better leave. I don't believe anybody will come here during the daytime. So we'll have to keep a close watch on this place after dark."

I'd been expecting to hear that. But it put a knot in my stomach just the same.

Brains picked up the broom and swept it over where we'd made tracks. Then, he replaced the broom in the exact position he'd found it.

As we left, I glanced in the direction of the old graveyard. I half expected to hear those awful sounds again. But there was only a dead silence, the kind you could almost cut with a pair of scissors.

"We'll return at eight-thirty tonight, Operative Three," Brains said, quietly.

I sure didn't want to. In fact, I was almost beginning to wish that school would start right away instead of in two weeks. That might give me an out from this case. I really wanted to get out before I was carried out with a lily in my clasped hands.

We'd just got into town when Stony Rhodes intercepted us. He gave Brains a sheet of paper with some names on it, maybe a dozen.

"One man I'd never seen before went into Mr. Beal's office," Stony reported. "He was tall and thin and had a long nose. He wore rimless glasses and was dressed all in black. He looked to me like a mean type."

"Ah," Brains said. "Did he limp slightly, Stony?"

"Yeah," Stony said excitedly. "He sure did. I remember now. . . . You know who it was, Brains . . . I mean Barclay?"

Brains nodded gravely. "Yes," he said. "Thank you very much for such a superlative job of surveillance, Stony. I won't forget it. Now, you'd better go. Identification with me could damage your value as a secret agent."

"Gee, yeah," Stony said.

He slunk away, keeping to the shadows.

"Did you really know that man he described, Brains?" I asked.

"Certainly," Brains said. "My mother introduced him to me yesterday. He's the new minister over at the Congregational Church. But I just couldn't tell Stony that."

That night, when Brains and I left Crestwood after supper, we took extra precautions. We headed in the opposite direction from our real destination. Then, we doubled back. It was eight o'clock when we came out on the old road that led to Lake Carmine.

Brains had studied the almanac and also got a full weather report. The forecast was for cloudy skies and possible thunder showers. There would be no moon. Darkness would set in early.

It did. By the time we had concealed ourselves behind a clump of elderberry bushes across the road from the root cellar, night had arrived.

It was pretty awful, waiting there, afraid to move lest you make a tell-tale rustle. A couple of times a screech-owl let loose just beyond the graveyard and both times I almost died. I saw Brains take something from his pocket and examine it. I just couldn't believe he'd brought along an automatic pistol.

"You're carrying a gun, Brains!" I whispered. "A gun!"

"It's a water pistol," Brains said. "It's loaded with lemon juice. Lemon juice in the eyes can be disabling."

We kept waiting. Nine o'clock. Nine-thirty.

It kept getting darker. I began to see and hear things that weren't really there. All of a sudden, Brains put a hand on my arm. He hissed, "Sh-h-h-h-h!"

For a few seconds I couldn't make out anything. Then it took shape against the faint light of the sky. A figure was coming across the field from the direction of the old graveyard. He wore some kind of a short coat and a visored cap. He was up to his knees in the tall grass and weeds. Every few seconds he stopped.

We tried not to breathe. The man came down the bank and made his way to the heap of stuff piled against the old root cellar. He did just what Brains had done that afternoon, then ducked in out of sight. I started to get up and Brains said, "Not now. Wait."

We heard a creaking sound like a heavy door opening, then a soft thud as if closing shut.

Brains stretched out flat on the ground, his right ear buried in the grass. "Let's see if we'll hear that sound, Operative Three," he whispered.

Twenty minutes went by. Then it came. That muffled, roaring sound that we heard the first time we'd come.

"No wonder it appeared to come from under the ground," Brains said. He got to his hands and knees. "Let's go, Operative Three."

My legs were as firm as jelly as I sneaked across the road behind Brains. We crouched down behind some more bushes until the sound stopped. Then Brains picked up a rock and threw it against the old iron wheel of the hayrake.

Creeps! It made a clanging sound that I was sure could be heard in Crestwood.

We froze there, waiting. Then we saw him. He came out of the piled-up junk in kind of a crouch. He kept turning his head every which way. He started to go back in. Then, I wrecked everything. There was a lot of goldenrod around the old ruins. And I guess that did it. Anyway, I sneezed! I sneezed louder than I'd ever done before in my whole life.

The man picked up a stick. He charged toward us.

Brains had his water gun leveled. "At him, Jimmy!" he said.

Then all three of us stopped stock still.

"You kids!" a familiar voice gasped.

The man was Ben Carlin.

15 SHOCKING SURPRISE

BEN DROPPED THE STICK AND GLARED AT US FOR A MINUTE. THEN he gave us a sickly grin.

"Now you know," he said. "No use trying to scare you away any more."

"We don't know anything yet," Brains said. "What's in there, Ben?"

"Come see," Ben said.

We followed him. He shoved the big doors open. Beyond was the old root cellar and right in the center of it was—a racing car.

There was a workbench in the place and a dim light came from a couple of bulbs dangling overhead. The wires led to a battery in the corner. A rubber tube was hitched to the exhaust pipe of the racer and was attached to an iron pipe sticking out from the back of the root cellar.

"Well, well," Brains said.

"You've got to keep my secret," Ben said, almost begging. "You know what my uncle promised when my mother died."

"About staying away from racing cars," Brains said. "We're not going to say anything, Ben."

"I've been workin' on this car in secret for over a year. I just have to finish it in time for that Middlebury race."

I was doing some thinking.

"You spotted us that night you were revvin' the engine up," I said. "Did you make that awful sound like a Banshee, Ben?"

Ben grinned sheepishly. "It was a mistake doing that. I should've known you were too smart to believe in ghosts."

He reached back into the corner where the battery was and pulled out a shiny globe of metal that looked like an old-fashioned automobile headlight. Only, instead of a lens, it had a kind of grill across the front. Two wires dangled from it as Ben held it up.

"The Crestwood Fire Department got a new engine a couple of years ago," said Ben, "and the Acme Garage bought the old one for the parts. I found this lying around the shop and figured it might come in handy up here."

Brains and I looked at each other. We'd been scared out of our wits by a siren off a fire truck.

Brains said, "You got somebody to scare us that night over by the graveyard. Correct?"

"Yeah: Joe Keely," Ben admitted. "He knows about this car. Had to buy some parts from him."

"He took a chance grabbing hold of Brains," I said.

Brains picked up something that was draped over an old barrel, held it up to let the light shine on it.

"This is the old navy raincoat Keely wore, isn't it, Ben?"

Ben nodded. Brains kept studying it.

"Joe was in the Navy at one time," Ben said. "You guys will swear you won't tell anybody about this, won't you? I sure would like to win that prize money and I know I've got a good chance. I'd like to be as great a driver as my dad was."

"We promised we wouldn't talk," Brains said. He bent over the engine Ben had been working on. "See you've got a new distributor and dual carburetor on this job."

"Almost every nickel I earned went into this car, Brains. I've got to see Mr. Beal about the rest of the insurance on the car that was stolen and ditched. It's a total loss. . . . I haven't paid my entry fee yet. I don't want to do it too soon or my uncle might find out and—"

"Jimmy," Brains said, abruptly. "Ben wants to get some work done. Let's get back to Crestwood."

I knew by the tone of his voice that he'd seen something I hadn't. He was as nervous as a cat passing a doghouse.

When we got to where we'd left our bikes, Brains said, "That old coat I was looking at, Operative Three. There was a name and serial number stenciled inside the collar. All sailors have to have that done."

"Joe Keely," I said.

"That's just it, it wasn't. The name in that coat was James Kohler."

"Keely could have bought it at an army and navy store," I said.

"I don't believe so," Brains said. "The initials are the same. J.K. He kept them without thinking. A man does not change his name without a reason!"

My jaw dropped. "Then *he's* the one who stole the money?"

"That's something we must determine. He's been in Ben's hidden workshop. He could have left that chunk of dirt from his shoes on the stairway to Mr. Beal's office. We know it came from the root cellar even without the little piece of insulated wire that was stuck in it. He also knew where Ben kept his old car."

I felt shivery like a hunter must who's getting close to where a tiger's hiding. Then I thought of that crazy letter. But Brains mentioned it before I could get the words out of my mouth.

"One thing puzzles me, Jimmy," he said. "Why would Keely send that letter to the police? What does he care about freeing Will Parslow from a robbery charge?"

"You got me," I said. "But, creeps, if Keely finds out we suspect him, he could get plenty rough."

Brains touched his throat gingerly. "Yes, indeed," he said.

My partner walked back and forth for a moment, his head lowered in deep thought.

"We could probably get a line on this man if we knew his home town," Brains said. "We may have to go to Chief Hadley for help. He could wire the Navy Department for the name of the place where James Kohler enlisted."

"That'd be just fine," I said. "You tell the Chief about Keely and how you found his coat out in the root cellar, and that he was the guy in the graveyard who chased us. So Chief Hadley and his men figure something is hidden out there, maybe the camp fund money. So they tear the old Gault place apart. And —bang!—Ben is out of business."

I was almost out of breath when I finished.

"You're right," Brains said. "We'll have to figure a way to get the information ourselves. We'll sleep on it tonight."

"That mattress of mine in the tent is hard enough without adding anything to it," I said.

At breakfast the next morning, Mom told me that she'd run into Mrs. Holzworth, the lady who'd given her that Scotch-taped twenty-dollar bill. That Mrs. Holzworth had been real smart all along. She'd told the police about the torn bill the minute she'd heard about the robbery.

"Which all goes to show," my mother said, "there's no sense worrying over things that *might* happen. They seldom do."

I wished I could believe her. But I knew for sure that things were going to happen to us—and not good things, either.

I was a little late reaching the lab. That was because of Stony Rhodes. As I left our house, I got wise that the little pest was shadowing me. He'd been trying for a long time to learn the secret of getting into the crime lab and I guess he figured he'd find out by following me. Well, I took him on quite a journey up and down side streets until I was almost dizzy. I finally lost him down by the river.

Brains was scribbling on a big piece of paper when I entered.

"I'm redesigning the electronic device for the garage doors," he said. "I want to surprise my father on his birthday."

Brains putting time in on a thing like that jolted me. I didn't care if the garage doors opened automatically when Professor Benton approached in his car or if they never opened. Only one thing mattered.

"What about Joe Keely?" I asked. "Or have you forgotten about him?"

"No, indeed," Brains said. "I've worked out a scheme concerning that gentleman. After breakfast I stopped in to see Ben and without seeming to be too curious, asked him about Keely. I mentioned that my father needed some seat covers for our car and that I wondered if he could save money if he bought them from Joe Keely. Well, Ben thought he might. He said that if my father couldn't contact Keely at his store in Middlebury, to try the Hotel Westmore."

"I don't see how that helps us," I said.

"You will in a minute," Brains said. "Do you remember a man named Wright who used to live here in Crestwood?"

"George Wright!" I said. "How could I ever forget him! The best ball player I ever saw."

George Wright was sure that. He'd once played first base for the Crestwood Colts which was a twilight semi-pro league team. He'd been a terrific hitter. One year he'd batted .386! And at the same time held the league's record for stolen bases.

I guess he'd been sort of my hero. And I'd felt awfully bad when Mr. Wright had got himself smashed up in an airplane accident. I went to see him when he was in the hospital. He'd never played ball again.

"What about Mr. Wright?" I asked Brains.

"He happens to be the day clerk at the Hotel Westmore," Brains said. "Where Joe Keely lives."

"I don't get the connection," I said.

"Simply this," Brains said. "In his work as day clerk, George Wright undoubtedly sees the mail Keely receives. I feel confident that Mr. Wright would jot down the post marks on letters that arrive for Keely—if *you* should ask him, Jimmy. After all, you knew him well."

"Yeah," I said. "I guess he'd do it for me. But what good will knowing post marks do?"

"It might indicate the city or town where Keely came from. And where he might possibly have been known as James Kohler."

"Hey!" I said. "Not bad. But that means another trip to Middlebury. And I don't know if my folks . . ."

Brains smiled. "Everything has been taken care of," he said. "My father is driving to Middlebury tomorrow morning. He's to be on a TV panel discussing *Higher Education and Its Effect on Crime*. Interesting subject. . . . Anyway, I am driving to Middlebury with him. So are you. My mother obtained your mother's consent via telephone while you were coming here."

That's how it worked out. But it was so hot the next morning when we left Crestwood that I almost wished I could stay home. What made it worse was the way Professor Benton drove. I mean, Brains' father might have had ancient history down pat but he was back in grade school as far as an automobile was concerned. I figured he was going to need a new transmission long before seat covers.

When we finally rolled into Middlebury, Professor Benton let us out four blocks from the Westmore and went on to the TV studio. Brains had told him he had some business to attend to. Not that the professor even heard him. I think his mind was flipping around with all the things he wanted to say on the air.

The Westmore was a second-rate hotel but not too bad. George Wright was on duty at the desk and he recognized me right away when we walked in. He'd put on so much weight I hardly knew him except for that great big grin and hearty, booming voice of his.

"Jimmy!" he said. "And Barclay!"

He knew Brains, of course, but not half as well as he did me.

We all shook hands. Then, Mr. Wright said, "I've been reading about you two in the paper and how you found that dummy in the stolen car. . . . What brings you up here—detective business?"

He laughed as if he didn't think that could be the reason.

"Yes it is, Mr. Wright," Brains said. "And it's something of a very confidential nature, too. Jimmy will explain."

"Well . . . uh . . ." I started. "Do you have somebody named Joe Keely staying here?"

"Yes, we do," Mr. Wright said. He was frowning a bit now. "What about Keely?"

I guess Brains could see I was sort of fumbling so he took over and told George Wright why we'd come.

"Well," Mr. Wright said, when Brains had finished. "I don't figure there's anything wrong in what you ask. It isn't like opening his mail."

He turned around and reached back to the mail board behind the desk. He took three letters from a slot.

"I just sorted the morning delivery," he went on. "These three pieces of mail came for Keely."

Mr. Wright put the letters down on the counter in front of us.

One letter was from New York. The other two were from Welton City.

"Welton City," Brains said. "Two letters from there isn't very conclusive evidence. Do you possibly recall, Mr. Wright, if Keely receives more mail from that city than any other?"

Mr. Wright tucked the letters back in the slot.

"Hold on now," he said, quickly. "Come to think of it, he does get a fair amount of mail from that town. Why, yes! I remember now I even spoke to Keely about Welton City one time. You see, I've always been soft on that place. It was there where I walloped three homers in a single game."

"Golly, yeah!" I said. "That was the game that won the Colts the championship."

I guess Brains was afraid Mr. Wright and I would get going on a long-winded gab fest on baseball because he cut in fast and said that Mr. Wright had given us exactly the information we needed and that he was sorry but we had to leave. And we did, after thanking Mr. Wright for what he'd done and getting his word that his lips were sealed.

I thought we'd have to go to the TV studio and wait until Professor Benton was through and then drive back to Crestwood with him. But Brains had made other plans, I was pleased to hear. His father was staying for dinner at somebody's house after the telecast and we were to return by bus.

The minute we hit Crestwood, we made for the lab. Brains got out his typewriter pronto and slipped in a sheet of our official note paper with BENTON AND CARSON INTERNATIONAL DETECTIVE AGENCY printed at the top. Then, he began to type. I stood behind him, reading the words as they came on the paper.

The letter was addressed to the chief of police in Welton City and went like this:

DEAR SIR:

We would appreciate any information you may be able to supply us as to the character, behavior and reputation of one James Kohler.

Kohler is approximately 35 years of age; of medium height; weighs approximately 175 lbs.; dark brown hair; pale blue eyes; long, thin face. It is believed that subject at one time served in the U.S. Navy.

Any information supplied will be treated in complete confidence. A prompt reply would be greatly appreciated by the officers of this agency.

Brains took the letter out of the machine and signed his name as president almost as big as John Hancock.

I felt pretty uneasy. "I hope the police in Welton don't get in touch with Chief Hadley asking for a line on *us*," I said.

Brains spread his hands. "The calculated risk we take."

I sweated out the next two days. I was sure glad I hadn't signed that letter until I realized that as secretary of the agency I'd be involved just as much as Brains if anything went wrong.

We heard nothing from Welton City or from the editor of *Road Racing* either. Then, just after breakfast on the third day I got a call from Brains. It was a good thing that I beat my mother to the phone. For Brains said, "Eruption on Mount Olympus!"

This was our current emergency call meaning, "Come quick!"

Only a rocket could've made it to the lab any faster. When I rushed in Brains was pacing up and down, a letter held open in his hand. His face was the color of last week's bread.

I knew then that this was the end for our brave new detective agency.

"What's happened?" I gasped, steeling myself. "Don't spare me. I can take the truth."

"We have a reply from the police in Welton City," Brains said. "They report that . . ."

He stopped and handed me the letter.

"Read it yourself," he said.

I took it. My knees were wobbling and little creatures with icy cold feet were racing up and down my spine. I forced my eyes to read the typed words. The message didn't say anything about us.

It was brief and to the point. James Kohler had once served a two-and-a-half-year sentence in the state penitentiary for grand larceny! He was an ex-convict!

16 SINISTER JOURNEY

I GROPED MY WAY TO A CHAIR AND SAT DOWN. I WAS SHAKING ALL over. Creeps! The only convicts I'd ever known had been in the movies and TV.

"Brains," I said, "this is too big for us. We'd better tell Chief Hadley."

"Now don't get excited!" Brains said. "We must view this with calm deliberation."

He started walking in great agitation.

"Anyway, we've got to warn Ben," I said.

"No!" Brains snapped. "That would be stupid. I have an idea that Joe Keely is backing Ben. He might even be paying his entry fee under his own name. Ben and Keely have to be partners or Keely wouldn't have gone to all that trouble scaring us away from the root cellar. And partners aren't supposed to keep secrets from each other."

I hated to admit he was right.

"We don't want to be like a lot of people we know in Crestwood," Brains went on. "Condemning Keely just because he's an ex-convict is wrong. Lots of men who serve time in jail go straight afterward."

"He tried to choke you to death," I reminded him.

"A joke," Brains said. "But I will admit we must consider him a suspect. It is clear, in the light of his prison record, why he changed his name."

"O.K.," I said. "But what do we do now?"

"We go to the Acme Garage and talk with Ben," Brains said. "I wish to determine just how close his relationship is with Joe Keely. If we appear casual we should not arouse suspicion."

Casual, he said. Appear casual! Creeps!

We found Ben back of the garage, scraping the old paint and rust from the left rear fender of his beat-up car. I couldn't help noticing the new radiator ornament on the hood and the shiny rear-view mirror on the driver's side of the car. You couldn't miss them any more than you could miss spotting a mother-of-pearl roof on a woodshed.

"Hi," Ben said.

Maybe I imagined it but he didn't seem too happy to see us.

I ran a finger over the winged mercury on the radiator cap. "Snazzy," I said.

"We were wondering a while ago when you were going to try out your racing car, Ben," Brains said. "We thought you wouldn't mind letting us watch."

"Shhhhh!" Ben said. He shot a nervous look toward the garage. "Keep your voice down, will you?"

Just then, Ben's boss, Mr. Murfee, came around the corner of the garage. He flipped up a grease-blackened hand in a greeting to us.

"How're you, fellas?" he said. "Been having tea with the Widow Pruett lately?"

He laughed and we pretended to. But the gags about us and the widow had worn awfully thin, I'll tell you.

After Mr. Murfee was out of earshot, Brains spoke again, this time in almost a whisper.

"We thought maybe you might be testing the job tonight."

"Not tonight," Ben said. "She's not quite ready yet. Anyway, I have to drive up to Middlebury tonight for Mr. Murfee and pick up a couple of truck tires."

I was keeping close watch on Brains and letting him carry the ball. How he expected to get any dope on the relationship between Ben and Joe Keely was beyond me. But I needn't have concerned myself.

"You're going up to Middlebury tonight!" Brains exclaimed. "Will you be seeing Joe Keely?"

"Well, yeah. That's where I'm going for the tires," Ben said, uneasily. "What's it to you?"

"Nothing, really," Brains said. "I just meant . . . well, you see I didn't tell my father about that bargain in seat covers he might get from Joe Keely. I thought I might buy him the seat covers myself as a birthday present."

Brains stopped suddenly as if he'd just got hit by a big idea.

"Say, Ben!" he let out. "How about me riding with you up to Middlebury tonight? Then I can look over the seat covers at Keely's."

Ben thought over the idea. "All right," he said, finally. "I guess it's O.K. Meet me out front at seven."

"And what about Jimmy coming along?" Brains asked before I could signal him to stop.

"Yeah," Ben said. He started back at his paint scraping.

"I don't think I can make it," I said.

"Of course, you can," Brains said heartily. He looked at his watch. "Hey, Jimmy, we'd better scoot. . . . See you later, Ben."

When we were out on the street, I turned to Brains.

"What's the idea of going up there?" I asked fiercely. "Are you nuts?"

"I don't believe so," Brains said. "Ben clearly wasn't going to do much talking about his pal, Keely. So, I jumped at the chance to observe the two of them together."

"Well, have fun," I said. "I'm not going."

Brains didn't seem to hear me. He began humming *The Farmer in the Dell*.

"Look," I said. "I could never get permission. Both my father and mother are sure to turn thumbs down on me riding forty miles to Middlebury with anybody, let alone Ben Carlin."

Brains still kept on humming that idiot nursery rhyme.

"I'll ask them," I said, desperately. "Then you'll see."

If I live to be two hundred, I'll never figure parents. When I got home for supper, I brought up the subject of the ride to Middlebury soon as we sat down. I found it hard to get my dad's attention. All he seemed to be thinking about was that the auditors had arrived unexpectedly and as head accountant he had to get back to the office.

Mom wasn't any relaxed listening post either. There was a hassle going on among the officers of the Garden Club over who had insulted old Mrs. Ambrose by turning down her rambler roses. Every few minutes the phone would ring and it would be some lady with the latest battle dispatch for Mom.

The upshot was that Dad said, "Ask your mother whether you can go, Jimmy, I just haven't time to make any decision."

And Mom said, "All right, all right, only be careful of the roses. . . . Oh, dear! What am I saying? . . . And there's that telephone again."

So I was with Brains, waiting by the garage at seven p.m. when Ben drove his beat-up car out of the lot. We piled in.

I didn't have to wonder why the butterflies were doing figure-eights in my stomach. The idea of having a cozy little get-together with an ex-convict wasn't my idea of how to spend an evening.

Ben didn't seem to be any fountain of joy, either. Usually he was full of talk and jokes. But tonight he didn't open his mouth unless we spoke to him. I felt he wished he'd never agreed to take us along. He gripped the wheel hard and stared straight ahead as if he were driving through a pea-soup fog.

"Won't your uncle stop you from racing, Ben, when he finds out your name is entered?" Brains asked.

"He won't find out," Ben said. "The car'll be entered in Joe Keely's name. And even if my uncle comes to the race he won't recognize me in a helmet and goggles and with dirt and grease on my face."

Brains nudged me. I figured it was his way of pointing out that Joe Keely had quite a stake in the Middlebury Road Race. It was like somebody owning part of a prize fighter.

I honestly don't know how that miserable old car made it to Middlebury. But it did and in pretty good time, too, thanks to Ben's slick driving.

We came to a stop alongside the curb in front of a store that had been modernized and had a shiny blue tile front with chrome trim. There were tires and spare parts for cars and gadgets on display in the window. A big sign overhead said:

HONEST JOE KEELY   Auto Parts & Accessories.

Two men were standing behind the glass door, looking out at us. And I mean looking hard and real nasty. I recognized one of them as Joe Keely. I didn't know the other man.

When we went inside, the man who'd been with Keely brushed past us.

"See you later, Joe," he said, pushing open the door.

He was a heavy-set, tough-looking man, not exactly the type you'd find in a church choir.

Joe Keely didn't seem too pleased by our visit. He sort of glowered at Ben.

"I told you I was coming up for those tires," Ben said. He acted nervous, almost afraid. "So here I am, Joe."

Joe nodded. He held a half-smoked cigar in his right hand. The cigar was out. He put the cigar in his mouth and lit it, his eyes on Brains and on me.

"Ha!" he said. "The detectives."

"Yeah," Ben said, defensively. "They wanted to come along."

Brains spoke up. "Good evening, Mr. Keely," he said, politely. "Ben told me you might have a bargain in seat covers. I'm shopping for a birthday present for my father."

"You came to the right place, pal," Joe Keely said.

There wasn't one thing right about this place, if you asked me. Oh, it was clean and trim with merchandise stacked neatly on shelves. But something was making my heart bump its way up to my throat. Maybe I was scared of Keely because of what I knew of his past and because of the bad time he'd given us out at the old Gault place. Or maybe it was that I felt in my very bones that real danger was here, so close that you could almost reach out and touch it.

But Brains! He acted as a cool as a cucumber in a deep-freeze.

"If you will show me some merchandise, Mr. Keely," he said, "I might be able to make a decision. We haven't an over-abundance of time as we must be back in Crestwood at a reasonable hour. After all, we youths must get our sleep, you know."

I almost gagged. Keely just blinked his eyes. Then he went to the rear of the store and began taking seat covers from a shelf. As he did so, Brains strolled to the front and looked at the various items on display in the window. I knew he was giving the whole place a quick once-over.

He was back at the counter when Joe Keely returned with an armful of auto seat covers. Keely dumped them down in front of Brains. There were many designs and color combinations and my partner began inspecting each of them carefully.

I stood beside him and made out that I was interested in the seat covers, too. But I was watching Keely out of the corner of my eye. He sidled out from behind the counter and joined Ben on the other side of the store.

I couldn't hear what Keely said but I just knew it wasn't anything pleasant. Keely acted plain mad and Ben's face sort of flushed up and he wet his lips. It seemed plain as could be that Ben was getting a bawling out for bringing us along.

Creeps, now I wanted out more than ever. But hurry Brains? Naw! He just went on taking his own sweet time inspecting those fool seat covers.

"Make up your mind, for Pete's sake!" I whispered to him. "Let's get out of here."

"Don't be impatient, Operative Three," Brains whispered back. He had a trick way of speaking without moving his lips. Like a ventriloquist. "I expect interesting developments."

I didn't have a chance to ask him what kind of developments for just then Keely's tough-looking friend came into the store.

"Lefty," Keely said, "roll out those tires for the Acme Garage and put 'em in Ben's car."

The bruiser named Lefty nodded. He went into the rear of the store. He came back rolling a truck tire which he took out through the front door. In a short while he returned and rolled out the second tire.

"Both of 'em in your car," Lefty finally reported to Ben Carlin.

Ben thanked him. Then, Ben called out, "What about it, Brains? Did you find what you wanted?"

Brains shook his head. "I'm afraid there isn't anything here that strikes me," he said. "I'm sorry, Mr. Keely."

Keely sneered. "That's O.K., kid," he said. "I like to waste time. . . . Now everybody beat it. I'm closing up."

He didn't have to urge me. I was glad to check out of there.

Ben was gunning the engine of his car in short bursts as if he was anxious to get going, too.

As we rolled away from the store, I glanced back. Joe Keely and his thuggish companion were standing in the open doorway. I heard Keely's friend call out,

"Have a safe trip."

The man seemed to think he'd said something very funny. For he started laughing. I didn't know why—not then.

About a mile out of Middlebury there was a steep hill with a sharp curve at the bottom. It was nicknamed Suicide Bend because so many people had whipped down the hill too fast and been unable to make the turn.

Just before we reached this hill, I noticed Ben's car start to shimmy and lurch a bit. But that wasn't too unusual for the old heap. Ben didn't seem to pay any attention to it. Instead, he gave her more gas.

"Stop the car!" Brains said suddenly.

"What?" Ben said. "What're you talking about?"

"Stop at once," Brains said. "There's something wrong."

Ben pulled to the edge of the road and brought the car to a halt.

"What do you mean, wrong?" he said.

Brains had the door open and he stepped out. I saw him bend and peer at the right front wheel.

"Look here," Brains said. "This wheel is loose."

Ben and I both scrambled out. At first Ben said it was just Brains' imagination. But when he examined the wheel his face got pasty white.

You know those metal lugs that hold the wheel and the tire to the hub—the ones you have to tighten with a special tool after you've changed a tire? Well, only two of them were in place. There should have been five!

"Blazes!" Ben gasped. "I just can't understand it. I checked over the car myself only last week. . . . If . . . if you hadn't made me stop, Brains, we could've had a bad smash-up."

Brains nodded. "At the bottom of the hill," he said. "As we made the sharp turn . . ."

Creeps! I could see us all piled up in the ditch.

I was quite sure Brains was thinking along the same lines I was. Those tire lugs hadn't come off by accident. I didn't say anything. Neither did Brains. And I had no idea if Ben had any such suspicions. He seemed mainly concerned with getting us back to Crestwood.

He pawed through a box of tools and stuff in the back of the car and miraculously found a couple of extra lugs that fit the wheel.

"If we take it easy, four lugs'll hold all right 'til we get back to Crestwood," he said as he spun the tire-tool.

When the lugs were tightened and Ben had made a quick check of the other wheels, we climbed back into the car and, at reduced speed, continued our journey home.

It was only after Brains and I were safely back in the tent at the rear of the Bentons' house that I learned the full story of what had happened.

"Yipes," I said. "How did you ever get wise that there was something wrong with that wheel just before we hit that hill?"

"I suspected it long before then," Brains said. "Even before we drove away from Joe Keely's store."

"Huh?" I said. "I don't get it."

"It was quite simple," Brains said, modestly. "You will recall that while Joe Keely was getting those seat covers, I walked to the front of the store to look at the window display. I noticed Keely's friend, Lefty, out at the curb where Ben had parked his car. Lefty was bending down by the right front wheel. I began to get suspicious then, but it wouldn't have done any good to say anything with Keely standing right there. There's no telling what he might have done. And I wasn't really convinced that Lefty had done anything to the car until it began to act up just before Suicide Hill."

I lay back on the camp cot. I don't believe I'd really allowed myself to think of what might have happened out there on the road from Middlebury to Crestwood. But now, pictures done in bright colors began flashing through my mind.

"Creeps!" I said to Brains. "We could've all been killed!"

"Or hurt," he said. "Then, of course, the wheel might've stayed on and nothing would've happened."

"A fat chance," I snorted. "Joe Keely and Lefty tried to finish us off."

"I doubt that the intent was lethal," Brains said. "I believe it was more to get us momentarily out of the way. . . . Anyhow, don't forget, we have no real proof that anybody tampered with the wheel."

"So the whole evening turns out to be a nothing," I said.

"Not at all," Brains replied. "We learned a good deal. For instance, it would seem that Joe Keely has been using Ben Carlin to gain something for himself. Now, Ben's usefulness may be over and he can be pushed aside."

I buried my head in the soft pillow. All of a sudden I was so doggone tired that I couldn't keep my eyes open.

"Do me a favor, will you, Brains?" I asked.

"Perhaps," he said, cautiously. "What is it?"

"The next time Ben Carlin offers to drive us anywhere," I said, "please take Stony Rhodes."

17 THE NARROWING TRAIL

To ME, ALL THE MYSTERY IN THIS CASE HAD DISAPPEARED. IT seemed all too clear that Joe Keely was the criminal. He'd stolen the camp fund money! He'd used Ben's car and run it into Boiling Pond after sticking the dummy inside. And he'd sent that strange note to the police, just to get everybody all mixed up.

I felt sure that this was the answer to everything. And I held to my opinion all the next day until after supper. Then, something happened.

Brains and I were in the lab when a buzzer on Brains' desk rasped into life. It was a signal that someone in the Benton house was calling over the private telephone line Brains had rigged.

It turned out to be the housekeeper, Mrs. Ray.

"Yes, Mrs. Ray," Brains said. "This is indeed Barclay Benton in the flesh and positively not a spectre."

I grinned. Boy, when Brains and the housekeeper got together, sparks flew.

But suddenly Brains wasn't grinning. "You what?" he said, almost shouting. "I'll be right over. This could be serious."

He hung up and jumped to his feet.

"Hey," I said. "What goes on?"

"That escapee from a booby hatch," he said. "She forgot to give me a letter that arrived this morning. She says it's from Canada—from Toronto!"

"*Road Racing!*" I let out.

"So I would surmise!" Brains was striding across the lab. "Wait here. I'll be right back."

The sliding panel in the wall swung open and Brains stepped through and disappeared.

It seemed ages before he returned. Actually it was less than three minutes.

He had a letter clutched in one hand when he stepped again into the lab.

"From the editor of *Road Racing?*" I asked.

"Yes."

"What did he say?" I asked, eagerly. "Is Joe Keely a subscriber?"

Brains walked to his chair and sat down. He seemed a little subdued, I thought.

"There is only one other subscriber to this magazine, besides myself, in the entire area around Crestwood and Middlebury," Brains said. "No, it isn't Joe Keely, Jimmy."

"Who on earth is it then?" I asked.

"Ben Carlin," Brains said.

It really shouldn't have been a shock, I suppose. Yet, it was.

"Then . . . then it was Ben Carlin who sent that letter!" I said.

"So it would seem," Brains said.

"But why would *Ben* send it?" I said. "Why?"

"There is one way to get the answer to that question," Brains said. "And that's to ask Ben himself."

Ben Carlin wasn't at the Acme Garage when we went there. And he wasn't at his uncle's, where he lived. Brains telephoned and Mr. Lufkin told him that Ben had gone out directly after they'd had dinner.

"Well, we both know where he went," Brains said.

I nodded. Then I took an extra-deep breath and said, "All right, let's go!"

We left Crestwood by a roundabout way. It was kind of cloudy and you could hear thunder away off. We reached the old Gault place a little before eight and crouched in the bushes across the gravel road.

"Why are we hiding this time?" I asked Brains. "Ben knows we know about this place."

"You're forgetting Joe Keely," Brains said. "If he's with Ben tonight I certainly wish to wait and question Ben another time."

Brains slapped at his leg. "Something's biting me!"

"Yipes," I said. I felt it now. "We're sitting on an ant-hill!"

We moved in a hurry. No sooner had we hunkered down behind an old juniper bush when we heard a sound that came from the woods back of the old graveyard.

"Ben's brakes," Brains whispered.

It wasn't too long before Ben sneaked across the field to the old root cellar, alone.

Brains said, "Okay, let's go, Operative Three."

Ben stopped as if shot when we came across the road.

"It's only us, Ben," Brains called.

"Gosh, you scared me for a minute," Ben said. His grin seemed forced. "Well, come on. Let's get out of sight in case somebody comes along."

It was pitch black in that root cellar when Ben closed the big wooden doors behind us. He snapped on the lights hanging from the roof. I saw the expression on his face as he looked at the racing car. No mother could've been prouder. He took a package from his pocket and, opening it, dumped some new spark plugs on the small bench near the racer.

"She's a beauty, huh?" Ben said. "She ought to do a hundred and forty easy on the straightaway."

Brains didn't fool around. He was all business.

"Ben," he said. He stood right in front of Ben Carlin, facing him. "We know it was you who sent that note with the pasted-up letters to the police."

Ben had picked up a wrench. Now it slipped from his fingers and hit the ground. His face got as pale as a daisy petal.

I think he was about to deny everything when Brains spoke again.

"We found out that you subscribe to the Canadian magazine, *Road Racing*, Ben. And we know that you cut some of the letters you used in that note from the title of that magazine."

Ben was breathing hard as if he'd run a quarter of a mile. He leaned against the racer, his hands out in front of him for support.

"All right," he said. "I won't lie. Yeah, I sent that note."

"Why?" Brains asked.

"Why did you go to all that trouble setting up that store dummy in Mr. Beal's office?" Ben threw back at Brains. "Then taking it to the courtroom. You wanted to help Will Parslow. Well, so did I!"

Brains nodded. "And you—yourself—most likely dropped that book of matches near where your old car was stolen, too."

"Sure," Ben said.

He tried to laugh but it was a failure. Tiny beads of moisture were on his forehead.

Nobody said anything for a while. Ben leaned down and picked up his wrench, then reached for the spark plugs.

"Got to get busy, fellas," he said. "I want her ready for a tryout in a couple of days."

"It'll be a tough race at Middlebury," I said. I just felt I had to say something. "Lots of good drivers."

"I'm going to win it," Ben said. "I've got to."

Ben had a small fan going but it didn't clear the air much. The light bulbs he needed took most of the juice of his battery. The smell in that old root cellar wasn't easy to take.

Brains again let Ben have it straight. "What do you know about Joe Keely, Ben?" he asked.

"Not too much," Ben said, guardedly. "But he's okay."

"That's not his real name," Brains said. "He's an ex-convict from Welton City and his name is James Kohler."

Ben's head snapped up as if it had been on a string.

"This is no surmise," Brains said. "We know for sure!"

"Well, he's not the only guy in the world that made a mistake," Ben said. He was getting mad. "You kids are going to get in a mess some day, snooping around like you do."

"We don't pry into things without a good reason," Brains said. "For instance—robbery!"

"Keely didn't do it!" Ben said. "You've got to prove he did before you come to me and—"

"We didn't say anything about Joe Keely being guilty," Brains said. "You did."

"Look," Ben said. "Take it easy with Joe. He's been helping me. Without him I'd never have had a chance to get in that race. Now leave me alone, will you?"

"Certainly," Brains said. He turned to go.

"I'm sorry, fellas," Ben said. "I shouldn't have got sore. You're only trying to help, I guess."

I didn't know what to say. So I just kept on not saying it.

Brains ran his fingers over the tread of one of the racing car's brand new tires.

"They cost something, Ben."

"Joe gave me credit," Ben said sullenly.

He swung the doors open for us and we made our way out.

"Well," I said as we started pedaling back to Crestwood. "I don't know where we stand now."

"Neither do I, Operative Three," Brains said. He seemed oddly cheerful. "We still don't know why Ben sent that note. But I believe we have started something fermenting."

"And that means?" I said.

"It means rather astonishing things will soon take place. The trail is narrowing, Operative Three. We cannot relax now even for a minute."

I didn't have to wait long for Brains' prediction about astonishing things happening to come true.

The very next morning when I reached the crime lab, Brains greeted me with, "Somebody stuck a note in the garage door last night!"

He pointed to a workbench where a piece of paper was spread out. Neatly printed in pencil was:

BENTON & CARSON DETECTIVE AGENCY. IT WILL BE TO YOUR ADVANTAGE TO WATCH WILL PARSLOW'S HOUSE TONIGHT. A FRIEND.

13 NIGHT WATCH

I'LL NEVER FORGET THAT DAY. IT SEEMED AS IF IT WOULD NEVER end. Brains and I kept asking ourselves just what the note could possibly mean. Was Will Parslow mixed up in this thing after all?

It began raining in mid-morning and the downpour continued without a let-up. We went to a movie in the afternoon but I couldn't have told you what it was all about when we came out. On our way back to the lab we passed the Acme Garage. We saw Ben's old heap parked close to the side of the building.

"That's funny," Brains said, slowing down.

"What?" I asked.

"I wonder what became of the do-dads Ben had on his car."

I noticed for the first time that the tricky radiator ornament on the hood was gone. So was the shiny rear-view mirror on the driver's side.

"Well, you'll have to admit they stuck out like sore thumbs," I said.

The rain finally stopped by supper time. We had my favorite chow, pot roast and noodles with thick gravy, but I just picked at it. Ann had come back from Lake Carmine the night before and she said Mom ought to take my temperature.

"Why didn't you stay at the lake?" I snarled at my sister. "It's been so peaceful around here. . . ."

"That's enough, Jimmy," Dad said. "When are you kids going to declare an armistice?"

"I'm willing to meet him at the summit . . ." Ann said, "and push him off."

"If you're going to sleep outside again tonight, Jimmy," Mom said, "better take an extra blanket. It's damp and foggy out."

Dad said it looked as if Chief Hadley and the police in Crestwood had just about given up on the robbery of Mr. Beal's office.

"It's terrible on the Parslows," my mother said as she started clearing the table. "Will Parslow will never be free of suspicion until the thief is found."

I felt whoozy inside. I dreaded to think of what Brains and I would learn that night. I could almost hear the Widow Pruett cackling with glee when they arrested Mr. Parslow again.

I watched television for a while. Then, around seven-thirty I left the house with the extra blanket under my arm. Brains was sitting on his cot in the tent wearing his high school warm-up jacket. He had heavy rubbers on his feet.

"We'd better arrange for the stakeout right away, Operative Three," he said. "We will go on foot. Reconnaissance on bicycles would be too conspicuous."

I nodded.

"You have your flashlight?"

I nodded again.

We left the tent and headed along Chestnut, then we turned down Madison, a narrow side street that took us to the lumberyard. We stopped near a corner where there was a high board fence and listened. You never knew about Stony Rhodes. Sometimes he came right up out of the ground or out of a tree trunk when you least expected him.

We crossed a big empty lot where the little kids played ball and came to the street where the Parslows lived.

The fog was as thick as mush. I was already soaked with perspiration when we turned into a short lane that led us around in back of the Parslows' clapboard house. Lights were burning inside. We crouched down behind the trunk of a big horse-chestnut tree and waited. We didn't really know for what.

"It could be another ambush, Brains," I whispered. I shivered, too.

Suddenly the back door opened and Johnny Parslow came out. He dumped something into a garbage can, then went back in again. I kept glancing over my shoulder at a row of honeysuckle bushes growing along an old picket fence.

I felt like a sitting duck, and told Brains so.

"We must see this through, Operative Three."

I know we waited for another hour. I was seeing myself propped up in bed with double pneumonia when a car went by in front of the Parslow house. It wasn't going very fast, most likely because of the fog. We saw its headlights groping ahead of it. Then it was out of sight.

"Somebody's taking us for a sleigh-ride," I said, after waiting another ten or fifteen minutes.

"Sh-h-h-h-h-h-h!" Brains warned. "Get down."

I sprawled out on the wet grass, my heart beating like a bongo drum. Then I heard a stick snap and a shoe crunch against gravel. I tried not to breathe.

A figure of a man took shape not fifty feet away from where we crouched. He stopped still and listened for a few seconds, then bent his head and moved toward a bed of flowers at the

corner of the Parslow house. Both of us knew it was the spot where Mrs. Parslow planted her nasturtiums.

The prowler got down on his knees and started scraping up dirt with his hands. Then he reached into his pocket and pulled something out. He put it on the ground, then began covering it over with dirt.

"Now, Brains?" I whispered.

"No! Wait!"

The figure slipped away. He had about time enough to get out to the street when Brains said, "All right, Jimmy! After him!"

We broke into a run. The prowler didn't hear us coming until he was close to where he'd parked his car. Just as he swung around, Brains stabbed the light beam right in his face.

"Hold it!" Brains said.

I sure got a shock. The prowler was no man. He was a kid, only a couple of years older than Brains and I, with a crew cut. He had a moon face and a jaw that was undershot, and a pair of eyes set kind of far apart. His mouth was popped open.

Brains had more than once reminded me that a mouse will get up on its hind legs and fight when at bay. That's what happened. The kid stopped being scared and he reached for a rock at his feet. I dived at him and made one of the best tackles I'd ever pulled off. Man, I sure cut him down. Then I rolled him over and got a hammerlock on him. I put on the pressure until he yelled uncle.

"Hold him there, Jimmy," Brains said and knelt down beside our catch. He played the flashlight on the kid's car. It was quite a hot rod, painted red and yellow.

"This was the car we heard go by," Brains said. "All right, let him up."

"I'll go to the Parslows and call the police," I said.

"N-no, please don't," Moon-face said.

"Not yet, Jimmy," Brains cautioned. "The reason I didn't want him jumped back there was because we can't let anybody know about this yet, even the Parslows."

We frisked our captive but found he packed nothing more deadly than half a candy bar.

"Go back there and dig up what he buried in the garden, Jimmy, will you," Brains said. "But don't make any noise."

I would get that job. On the way back, I wondered if Will Parslow had a shotgun in the house loaded with rock salt—or worse.

I didn't have much trouble finding where the stuff was buried. When I uncovered it, I gave it a quick treatment with the flashlight. It was a long, bulky, white envelope with rubber bands around it.

Suddenly I stopped breathing. My heart sounded like an African jungle combo for a few seconds, and I flattened to the ground. A window slid up. I heard Mrs. Parslow's voice. "What's the matter, Will?"

Ever stop breathing for a whole minute? It makes your ears ring. Finally the window slammed down, and I didn't lose a split second getting away from there.

Our captive was huddled against the side of the hot rod when I got back. He had tears in his eyes and he was holding on to his right arm.

"He got ideas again," Brains said. "I had to use some judo on him."

I handed Brains the envelope and he took the rubber bands off. Then he brought out a bunch of bank checks, held together by some string. He put the light beam on them, and gasped.

"The checks all seem to be made out to the Community Camp Fund!" Brains said. "They're the ones that must have been taken in the robbery!"

"Look, you guys," our prisoner said, "I didn't know what

they were. A guy just paid me five dollars to come here and—"

Brains shoved the checks into his pocket. "Okay, hand over your car keys," he said to Moon-face. "We're going to take a little ride."

"Give me a break. I was just trying to make a few bucks, like I said." Moon-face was sure scared. "If my folks find out, they'll kill me."

"A slight exaggeration, I'm sure," Brains said with a cold smile. "Jimmy, make sure he stays put in the back seat."

"He will if he doesn't want to get conked with a flashlight," I said.

"Boiling Pond would be an appropriate place for interrogation, don't you think, Jimmy?"

"I agree, Brains. And this character had better not act the dummy."

"Y-You wouldn't kill me?"

"Don't tempt us," I said, putting on a nasty laugh. Ha! I'm the guy who always feels guilty when he steps on a bug by mistake.

We didn't go to Boiling Pond. We didn't drive anywhere. Moon-face broke down completely. He said his name was Eddie Bixon and that his father was part owner of a furniture store in Middlebury. His mother was president of the P.T.A.

"All right, who got you to plant this stuff in Will Parslow's garden?" Brains asked, sharply. "It was Joe Keely, wasn't it?"

"G-gosh, how did you know?" Eddie Bixon asked.

"Just say I'm psychic, Eddie," Brains answered.

"Huh?"

"You'd better talk English to him, Brains," I said. "Or turkey."

"Joe Keely called to me when I was passing his store," Eddie Bixon explained. "He wanted to pull a gag on a guy, he said. Well, I was going for a ride anyway and I needed gas money. It sounded screwy but I told him I'd do it."

"What'll we do with him, now, Brains?" I asked.

"I think he's learned his lesson," Brains said. He looked at Eddie Bixon. "You know what might happen to you if Keely ever found out that you'd squealed. I believe that is the parlance crooks use."

"Yeah," Eddie said. "I'd be in a real jam."

"What do you hear about Keely in Middlebury, Eddie?" I asked.

"A lot of guys think he's a crook. Once, the police nearly pinned a stolen car rap on him."

"You have cooperated fully, Eddie Bixon," Brains said. "Keely can't prove you told us anything. He'll just have to wonder why his frame—er—gag didn't work."

"Then, you're going to let me go? Gee, thanks, you guys."

"If Keely does get tough with you," Brains said, "go right to the Middlebury police, Eddie, and tell them everything you know about him."

"You can bet I will. Sa-a-a-ay! Are you those two detectives, Benton and—?"

"Carson," I said, and nodded.

It was getting close to ten o'clock when Eddie Bixon got behind the wheel of his hot rod and drove off.

After he was gone, I said, "Brains, we'd better take those checks to the police."

"Not yet," Brains said. "It would ruin all the detective work done by our agency. We promised Eddie we wouldn't get him mixed up in it."

"How long do they keep kids our age in jail before they parole them?" I asked.

Brains didn't seem to hear me. He was thinking out loud. "It's all still quite a puzzle. First, Ben Carlin writes the police Will is innocent. Then somebody writes a letter tipping us off that Keely is planting evidence that Will did it."

"Keely is our man," I said. "We have to get the goods on him." I swallowed a big lump in my throat. "If he doesn't kill us first."

It didn't take long for the story to spread all over town the next morning, even before it appeared in the *Crestwood Daily Ledger*. It was on the local news broadcast at ten o'clock sharp and Brains and I were listening.

Mrs. Parslow had visited Chief Hadley at the police station and reported vandals had ruined her nasturtium bed. It must have happened sometime during the night. She said there were tracks in the soft dirt made by big square-toed shoes and she was certain the police had been searching the grounds and had trampled her nasturtiums flat.

" 'We are fed up with this persecution,' " the newscaster quoted her as having said. " 'If it doesn't stop, we'll sue the town!' "

Mrs. Parslow was usually a mild sort of person. She sure must have been burned to a crisp. She told Chief Hadley he had a one-track mind and that it looked as if the whole police force wasn't smart enough to corner an elephant in a telephone booth.

I had to laugh even though I was plenty scared.

"If the police searched the Parslow property last night," Brains said, "that means that somebody tipped them off. Most likely Joe Keely. He is probably wondering right now why Will Parslow hasn't been arrested again."

I nodded and swallowed a lump the size of a tennis ball that came up in my throat. "Keely's going to go after somebody," I said. "Most likely us."

"We will be ready for him, Operative Three."

The only thing I could think of right then was how often buses ran from Middlebury to New York or San Francisco and if I had enough in the bank to buy a ticket.

"Keely has no reason to suspect us, Jimmy," Brains said. "Right now I'll bet he believes the police did find those checks but don't want to make a move yet. Keeping suspicion on Will Parslow, he figures, will keep the hunt for the stolen money here in Crestwood."

I wish I hadn't seen so many TV shows. I wondered how it would feel to be sitting inside a big cake of cement at the bottom of Boiling Pond.

Why, oh why, hadn't they tried to raise the money for that Community Camp Fund five years ago?

19 POLICE WORK

Brains and i rode past the acme garage just after lunch.
Brains thought Ben might volunteer some new information if
he saw us. But we didn't run into Ben. Instead, a police car
pulled up alongside. Officer McKeon was driving.

"I've been looking for you two," he said. "Chief Hadley wants
to talk to you."

Brains said, "How interesting."

I couldn't get a peep out of me. Even though I'd half expected to be arrested, it hit me like a ton of bricks.

When we walked into Chief Hadley's office Lew Jarman, of
the *Ledger*, was there.

"Sit down!" the Chief snapped.

You'd think McKeon had just brought in public enemies one
and two. I never saw Chief Hadley more steamed up. His triple
chins were shaking like molded jelly.

"Of course, you know what happened last night," the Chief
said. "We got a tip there was something hidden in Mrs. Parslow's flower bed. When we got there it had been dug up. Why?"

"Why do you ask us, Chief?" Brains asked.

"I'll tell you why, Benton! I'll bet you and your sidekick here had something to do with it!"

"I should warn you, sir," Brains said, "I do not believe my father would like it very much if he heard you made these accusations."

Chief Hadley calmed down a little. He pawed at his face with his hands and let loose with a little groan. Then he stabbed a finger at us.

"Where were you two around ten o'clock last night?"

"Sitting in a car talking to a kid we know from Middlebury," Brains said. "We can prove it."

"Why don't you do some of the answering, Carson?" the Chief yelled at me. "Why are you clamming up?"

"Brains is my superior," I said. "He is the president of the Benton and Carson—"

"Oh, be quiet!" Chief Hadley said.

He got to his feet and started pacing the floor, his hands clasped behind his back. His cigar was shooting sparks and was practically chewed to a frazzle. I was tempted to warn him his chewing tobacco was on fire.

"First you two kids discover a corpse that turns out to be a store dummy," the Chief raved. "Then a wild man nobody else sees chases you out of a graveyard! . . . Then you haul that dummy into court and—Listen you two! If I can ever prove you're interfering in police business, I'll send you away until you're eligible for an old age pension!"

"Yes, sir," Brains said most politely. "And please do not forget that if our agency can help you in any way, just let us know."

Lew Jarman grinned and Chief Hadley caught him at it. He chased Lew out along with us.

Outside the station house Jarman said, "If you guys are up to something, watch your step."

The reporter was serious. So were Brains and I when we arrived back at the crime lab. I was sure that Brains was thinking just what I was thinking. Namely, that we had evidence that belonged to the police.

"There are such things in our line of business, Operative Three," Brains said after some deep thinking, "as extenuating circumstances."

I made out that I knew what he was talking about.

"Only Eddie Bixon could prove Joe Keely wanted those checks planted in the Parslow nasturtium bed," Brains went on. "Which means that Eddie could get into a mess himself. We promised to protect him. Hasty action on our part might put him in the work farm over at Rumford."

"So far you've sold me," I said.

"If we tell all we know now and Keely is arrested, what becomes of Ben's racing car?" Brains said. "Especially if some of the parts, or the tires on the racer are—to use the vernacular —hot? Ben has set his heart and soul on winning the Columbus Day race. I'd say at the moment that we're justified in protecting the innocent."

"You make it sound okay," I said. But I wasn't too sure.

Anyway, we left it that way. But Brains knew as well as I did that the ice we were skating on wasn't thick enough to hold up a chickadee. And that's a mighty small bird.

"We know Keely is the robber," I said. "But how in blazes are we going to catch him with the money?"

"I admit I have no plan, Jimmy," Brains said. "We can't break into his store or search his hotel room. For that matter he could have it hidden anywhere."

My partner started walking back and forth. "Keely will slip up somewhere," Brains said. "We'll just have to wait and watch. When he does slip up, we act. There's just one thing we must be careful of . . . that's being followed by the police. I'll give odds that Chief Hadley has ordered that our movements, especially at night, be watched."

"They'll be wasting their time tonight," I said. "We've got to go to that church supper."

Brains grinned. "So we do. So we do."

When we got to the church we found that a mob had turned out for the supper.

"This could easily be the night Ben tries out his racer," I told Brains as we got a second helping of roast beef.

"Sh-h-h-h-h," he said.

I looked up and saw Chief Hadley walking past our table. His wife was with him. The chief gave us both a look that should have taken my appetite away but didn't.

Brains and I were so stuffed we thought we'd take a stroll outside and let the roast beef settle. We hadn't walked halfway across the parking area behind the church when Brains said, "Don't look now, but somebody's following us."

We wormed our way through the parked cars, came out into Oak Street, then stopped near a big lilac bush. The man following us didn't see us in the dark.

When he passed us, Brains said, "Good evening, Officer McKeon. The breeze is strong tonight. So are those peppermints you are chewing."

"Why—er—it's you, Benton," Officer McKeon said.

"When you shadow somebody, especially across a graveled surface, Officer," Brains said, "you shouldn't wear those heavy police shoes."

"I was going for cigarettes," the policeman said peevishly and walked away from us.

"You see what I mean, Operative Three?" Brains said. "We'll have to be extra vigilant."

I was mowing the lawn the next morning when Ann came out of the house and called to me.

"You got a message from outer space, Jimmy," she said. "Or from Barclay. *'Satellite Zeta is in orbit.'*"

It was an emergency. I lost no time getting over to the crime lab. Brains handed me a copy of yesterday's *Crestwood Ledger* the minute I arrived. He was sure upset.

"We missed seeing this item," he said.

The paper had been folded back to page 17. Brains had marked the item with pencil or I mightn't have found it, it was that small.

MIDDLEBURY USED CAR DEALER ARRESTED
Police Allege 'Honest Joe'
Keely Has Stolen Cars
in His Possession.

"Yipes," I said. "That could sure spill the beans."

Brains sat down in his official chair and agreed that it could. You don't often see Brains Benton looking a little beat.

20 THE PAYOFF

I GUESS BRAINS AND I WERE THE ONLY PEOPLE IN CRESTWOOD, outside of Ben Carlin, who paid much attention to that story. Folks in town mostly skipped over Middlebury news.

"Let's not be too discouraged, Operative Three," Brains said. "I've been thinking this over. Joe Keely is a veteran crook. He won't admit to anything unless they prove things on him."

"Ben's going to be scared out of his wits," I said.

Brains nodded, "We must have a talk with him."

We hopped off our bikes at the Acme Garage and waited until Ben finished wiping a customer's windshield. When he came over to us he didn't have to tell us he knew about Joe Keely. Ben looked like he'd just got out of bed from having a bad case of flu.

"We read about Joe Keely," Brains said.

Ben glanced around to see if anybody was within earshot. "I guess you kids were right about him," he said. "Gosh, I hope I don't get dragged into it. If some of that stuff I bought from him—well, like those ornaments I had on my old car and . . ."

"You got them from Keely?" I asked.

"Sure. Then he phoned and said I'd better ditch 'em. And not to ask questions. Or else!"

"Or else what?" Brains asked sharply.

Ben didn't answer right away. He looked all befuddled as if he didn't know quite what to say.

"I . . . I guess he meant maybe he'd refuse to finance me any longer with the racer," Ben stammered out.

If Brains was puzzled at what Ben had said or the way he'd said it, he didn't show it. In fact, my partner seemed to act a lot friendlier to Ben than he had before. I had a sneaking suspicion that Brains was going into his softening-up routine. I'd seen him work it before.

"I wouldn't worry too much about Joe Keely, Ben," Brains said, airily. "He isn't likely to spill anything to the Middlebury police. Not yet anyway. Perhaps he'll even get himself a smart lawyer and worm out of everything."

Ben shook his head. "Maybe, but I wish I'd never been fool enough to give him that. . . ." Again Ben stopped in confusion and his face got red. "I mean to get in debt to him. I've agreed to give him half the prize money if I win or come in second."

It wasn't a very hot day but Ben kept mopping his face with a towel.

"How's the racer coming along?" Brains asked abruptly.

"O.K.," Ben said. "O.K."

"Jimmy and I would certainly like to see you try it out," Brains said, pleasantly. "Do you expect to soon?"

"Maybe tonight," Ben said.

"Good!" Brains said. "I just know you'll let us witness the occasion."

"Well, I guess it'll be all right," Ben said, uncertainly.

"It might be a good idea if we drove out there with you, Ben," Brains said. "You might like somebody around in case

Joe Keely showed up. . . . Not that he will, understand. After all, he's in jail."

It didn't take any great power of observation to see the fear that flashed across Ben's face.

"Yeah," he said. "You fellows ride out with me. I'll . . . I'll let you know when I'm going to leave."

"We'll be in our tent from seven to eight," Brains said.

When we got back to the crime lab, I read the account of Joe Keely's arrest again. This time slowly. The Middlebury police claimed they had witnesses who could prove Keely received goods that had been stolen. And Keely was quoted as stating that he was sure who they were. They were kids who were getting back at him because he'd caught them trying to steal things in his used car lot and he'd threatened to go to their parents.

"If they do find him guilty when the trial comes up, you think he'll confess to the robbery here, Brains?"

"Of course not," Brains said. "He'd just get a heavier sentence. And he would like to have some ready cash waiting for him when he got out of prison again."

"By that time, maybe, we'll be graduated from high school and in college somewhere," I said. "I hope."

Brains was clearly in one of his silent thoughtful moods, so I didn't stick around. I left him working on that wristwatch transistor radio of his.

I never spent a longer day. I listened to a ball game, then started cleaning up the basement until around supper time.

Dad was going to a lodge meeting that night and Mom was having some sort of committee meeting and Ann had a date so nobody brainwashed me while I ate.

I got to the tent a little after seven. Brains told me Ben had already been there. He would pick us up in about a half hour in front of the Acme Garage.

Ben was putting some oil in the crankcase of his old heap when we got there. Just as we got under way, Brains said, "Ben, drive in the direction of Middlebury. Keep on that road until we're sure no one is following us."

"Not a bad idea," Ben said.

We'd gone about six miles when Brains motioned to Ben to pull into a side road. Brains sure was in command.

"We'll wait a couple of minutes," he said, "and make sure."

Some cars went by but they were in an awful hurry. Then we swung onto the road again and went back toward Crestwood for a couple of miles before we turned into the road that would take us to the old Gault place.

A half hour later we got out of the car near a thick woods and followed Ben through it until we came to the graveyard. We waited there for a few minutes, watching and listening, before we crossed the field to the root cellar. The place still gave me the shivers. Creeps! It seemed even spookier than it had before.

It was dark and damp inside the secret garage and I was glad when Ben got the light bulbs burning.

The racing car didn't have the body on it yet. I got into one of the bucket seats and jiggled the gear handle. "I sure would like to start that engine up, Ben," I said.

Ben Carlin took after his dad, all right. This was quite a job he'd done. The racer had tubular framing and front suspension.

"The gears are a little slow between first and second," Ben said. "There's a tendency to understeer when you're taking a corner. I've been working on the brakes mostly the last couple of times. They shudder a little." He shoved the ignition key into the lock. "Start her up."

"Me?" I said. Then I turned the key and pressed the starter. Yipes, what a roar! No wonder we'd heard it from a distance that night. It was a Jaguar engine, and a real beauty.

Ben cut the ignition and said there was time to get the body on before midnight if we'd help him. He didn't want to chance running it on the road until then.

Of course, we pitched in. It was so hot in the root cellar that in no time at all Brains and I were soaked to the skin.

We'd just got the hood on when I heard the sound. The creak of a rusty hinge. I looked over my shoulder just as one of the wooden doors swung inward. I saw a man come in. I tried to yell but no sound came from my throat. I was petrified.

Brains and Ben were bending down at the rear of the car when the voice said, "All right, everybody. Stay right where you are!"

It was Joe Keely!

Brains and Ben stood up. Ben stared at Keely, his mouth open.

"What's the idea, Joe?" he finally choked out.

"Drop the wrench, bright boy," Keely said to Brains, and moved in closer. He held a wooden club the size of a leg of lamb. "I got out on bail, Ben. A thousand dollars. I don't figure to go back to Middlebury."

Joe Keely looked like a criminal now. His eyes were hard as rocks and his lips were curled back from his teeth.

"J-Joe," Ben said. "Don't take—"

"Back, all three of you," Keely said and waved the club at us. "Against the wall there in back. Move!"

We bunched together and did what he said.

"Soon as they find I've got a record," Keely said, "what chance would I have, huh?"

Then Joe Keely reached toward an old auto tire that hung from a peg on the wall just opposite from where we stood, all the while watching us like a hawk.

"No, Joe," Ben said desperately. "Don't take that! You can't do that to me!"

Keely laughed. When his hand came out from groping inside the old tire, it held a thick envelope. "I'll need to pay myself back that thousand, Ben. With interest!" he said.

Keely started backing toward the door, and that club he held began to look bigger and bigger to me.

"The Camp Fund money!" Brains said.

I gulped like a goldfish. It had to be!

"Keely, you won't get away with it!" Ben choked out.

"Shut up!" Keely said. "Don't any of you move a step, or I'll let you have it!"

We knew he wasn't bluffing. We stayed frozen. Nobody wanted a fractured skull.

Keely ducked down and backed out. When he slammed the doors shut, we all unfroze and dashed forward. I didn't get far. I tripped over a toolbox and plowed up some dirt with my chin. When I got to my feet I saw Brains and Ben pushing at the doors. They were too late. I heard a padlock click shut, and Keely's laugh.

We were locked in!

21 GETAWAY!

I DON'T THINK WE SAID A WORD FOR ALMOST A MINUTE. THEN Brains and I looked at Ben. I never saw anybody appear so sick and still be on his feet.

"You knew the money was hidden here, Ben," Brains finally said.

Ben nodded.

We could hear a car's engine racing outside.

"We have to pull ourselves together," Brains said. "We must think calmly in this emergency. First things first. For instance, we must find a way out of here."

I tried to think but couldn't.

"The car, Ben," Brains said. "It could break that door down. Let's get it started."

Ben shook his head. His face was covered with beads of sweat.

"There's all that junk outside. One piece is an old mowing machine. We'd wreck the racer." He leaned against his old workbench, pounding at it with his fist. "What a fool I was!"

169

Brains walked around, studying the inside of the root cellar. I noticed him inspecting the low roof carefully, particularly an overhead beam that Ben had propped up with a pair of two-by-fours.

From outside the sound of the engine racing continued.

"I think Keely must have parked his car in the soft sand," Brains said. "From the sound, I'd guess that he's stuck. That gives us a little time."

Brains pointed to the ceiling. "Ben, that beam you've got propped up, how rotten is it?"

Ben seemed to get a grip on himself. He followed the direction of Brains' pointing finger.

"Pretty rotten, I'd imagine," he said. "Those beams have been there a long time holding up about two feet of dirt and sod."

"Rotten enough to collapse if we knocked out that prop?" Brains said.

Ben's eyes brightened as he caught what Brains meant. He groped under his work bench and came out with a sledge-hammer.

"Stand clear," he said. Then, he swung the hammer and knocked the two-by-fours loose.

I had my body pressed against the side of the root cellar near the door. I heard the old beam creak and groan. It started to sag and some clods of dirt and a couple of stones nearly clobbered Ben before he ducked out of the way.

"I think if we try hard enough," Ben said, "we can poke a hole up through there in less than an hour."

Brains held up a hand for silence. We listened. From outside came sounds that told us Keely still hadn't got out of the soft sand.

"Hurry," Ben said. "He knows I've got my old car parked back of the graveyard. He'll get away in that."

The three of us worked like beavers, poking at the roof with the long two-by-fours. We'd jab and then dodge the stuff that fell away from the roof. There wasn't much air in the cellar fit to breathe after a while. We were all gasping like we'd just swum the English Channel. I had dirt in my hair and in my eyes, and a lump on my head from a rock I'd forgotten to duck.

The last time we'd stopped to rest, we couldn't hear a sound from outside.

"He's gone for my car!" Ben said. "It'll take him a few minutes to get there. And that heap won't hit over forty and not that for very long before the rear end falls out. We still have a chance, you guys."

While we worked, one thing became very clear to me—and I knew to Brains, too. Ben must have known the money was hidden in the root cellar all the time. That meant that he'd been in on the robbery with Joe Keely. Now Keely was crossing him and getting away with the money.

"Soon as we get out of here and pull that stuff away from the door," Ben said between gulps of air, "we'll go after Keely!"

"Where's he headed?" Brains asked. "Do you know?"

Before Ben could answer, a great shower of dirt came down. Then we saw the hole up there—and stars in the sky.

"Come on!" Brains yelled. "All we have to do is widen it enough for one of us to slip through. The other two can stand on the bench and boost him up."

"I'll go," Ben said, excitedly. "I'm pretty thin, and I have a key to that padlock." He fished a big, old-fashioned key out of his pocket and stood looking at us.

Brains' face was expressionless.

"Okay," said Ben with a sigh, "I know how it must look to you fellows. I could take off once I got outside, and be long-gone before anybody found you in here. But it's not like that at all. I . . . Oh, there's no time to explain now! Here!" He tossed the key to Brains.

Ben and I got Brains on our shoulders and lifted him up. The workbench was wobbly under us and for a couple of seconds I thought we'd all come down with a crash. But Brains wriggled through the hole in the roof and disappeared. A moment later he had taken the padlock off the doors and swung them open.

It took all our strength to pull that old rusty farm machinery clear of the door. We had to rest for a few minutes after that. I thought my heart would jump right through my ribs and sail across the gravel road.

"Where is Keely going, Ben?" Brains asked again, when we'd caught our breath.

"He won't go to Middlebury," Ben said. "And surely not to Crestwood. I'm guessing he'll make for the airport at Conway. You can hire planes there. Like I said, he can't go very far in that old heap."

Ben got into the driver's seat and Brains climbed into the bucket beside him.

"That rubber tube attached to the tailpipe, Jimmy," Ben said. "Yank it loose!"

I didn't waste any time. Then Ben turned that Jaguar horsepower loose and the roar must have been heard in Crestwood.

"Climb on the back," Ben yelled back at me.

We slid out of the root cellar, Ben making sure he didn't get the tires in the soft sand. He picked up speed when we were out on the hard gravel but not too much.

The concrete road to Conway crosses the old Lake Carmine road a few miles before the lake itself. Then it's about eleven miles to the airport.

After what seemed like hours, Ben slowed for the turn onto the concrete road.

"You know now. I stole that money."

He was going up through the gears and I had to hang on. I

had both arms around the back of Brains' bucket seat, and my feet braced against the framework behind. That Jaguar was roaring now and the trees and fields on each side were just a blur.

"Sure," Brains said.

"I was going to give most of it back," I heard Ben say.

After that, talk wasn't of any use. The wind picked words up and threw them far behind us before they could be heard. Yipes, we were traveling.

Man, could Ben drive! He judged the curves perfectly and had those tires glued to the road. He could have won the Middlebury race easy that night.

I gritted my teeth and hung on for dear life when we took another S curve. Then he really began to pour on the coal and I saw the needle of the speedometer point to 130 miles per hour. *Yipes!*

We zoomed past a side road. I was sure I caught a glimpse of a police car parked there. I twisted my head around a few seconds later and saw a pair of headlights. They'd never catch up with us, not until we got to the airport. When I looked around again I nearly got jolted loose from the racer. We must have hit a spot where repairs had been made in the road. I couldn't see the headlights back there now.

The drivers of the cars we passed must have thought we were maniacs riding a jet plane without wings. Once Ben had to swing wide to make a curve and I was certain the wheels on my side missed a wooden fence-rail by only an inch.

My throat was as dry as a bone. I'd been soaked in sweat when I'd climbed aboard and now I felt as if I'd been taken out of a deep freeze.

Suddenly I heard a yell from Ben before it was whipped away by the wind. He braked the racer and I thought I'd go through the windshield along with Brains.

We slowed down and Brains pointed toward the tail-light of a car about three hundred feet ahead. It was headed for the ditch. We knew Joe Keely was in it even before he jumped out and headed for the woods.

Ben stopped the racer not more than fifty feet away from the abandoned car. When he jumped from behind the wheel, Brains shouted at him, "Remember, he's dangerous!"

The roar of the Jaguar engine still clogged my ears when I raced after Ben and Brains for the woods. But even so, I still was sure I heard the siren of a police car.

We stopped at the edge of the pine woods and listened. Keely certainly had never been a boy scout. He was making as much noise going through the underbrush as a frightened moose.

"He'll attack if we get too close, believe me," Ben said.

"We must use strategy," Brains told him. "I've camped in this district. I know it well. The Little Elk River that runs through here is too deep for Keely to cross. He'll have to skirt the bank and keep headed toward Conway."

Ben wasn't offering any suggestions. He was leaving it all to Brains.

"Listen," Brains went on, "you two follow him; I'll go off on an angle to the bank of the river. Simple geometry will get me there first."

Oh, brother. Math at a time like this!

"All right, let's move!" Ben said. "Find yourself a big club or something, Jimmy."

We could still hear the noise Keely was making, but it wasn't as loud as it was at first, of course. Ben and I headed in that direction and Brains cut off to the left. I got hold of a hunk of a limb and held it.

It was dark in the woods and I was shaking. Creeps, was I. Every once in a while we'd stop and listen.

"What's on Brains' mind?" Ben asked, when we were crouched behind a big rotted stump.

"I dunno," I said. "I only hope he knows."

About fifty yards further on, we heard the sound of swift water. Then, I saw a shape against the dark. A man's shape. Joe Keely!

He'd heard us coming. "Stay clear of me!" he yelled. "I warn you!"

I dropped flat. So did Ben. Then, we waited.

Just as Brains figured, Keely started moving along the river bank toward the left, in the direction of the airport.

"Come on," Ben whispered, and I saw he had a big rock in his hand.

We got to the river bank and followed Keely. The branches of the trees hung over the bank in most places and shut out what light was in the sky. I was glad the moon was the size of a clipped fingernail. We had to be extra careful. In some places brooks fed into the river. They were really small gullies. We crossed a couple of them and then caught sight of Keely about fifty yards ahead.

I kept on worrying about Brains. Where was he? How did he ever expect to handle Keely alone?

All of a sudden, I heard Joe Keely let out a scream. He disappeared right before our eyes. It was as if the ground swallowed him right up.

"Come on, Jimmy! You, too, Ben! We've got him!"

It was Brains' voice.

We broke into a run and in a moment reached the edge of one of those gullies. This one was too wide to jump across. There was a log that spanned it from bank to bank.

The gully was at least seven feet deep and it was filled with rushing water. I looked down and then it was that I saw Joe Keely—or his head, at least. The man was floundering in the water, beating his hands and gasping for breath as he fought to keep himself afloat.

Brains suddenly emerged from the deep shadow on the far bank of the gully.

"We'd better go and get him before he drowns," Brains said.

Ben and I slid down the bank on our side and Brains went down the one on his. Keely tried to put up a fight. But he was all in and Ben had no trouble dragging him out and up the bank. We all looked like drowned rats.

Brains took the package of money from Keely's pocket. It was soaking wet but it would dry out.

"Boy, it was lucky he fell off that log," I said.

"There was not one bit of luck in the occurrence," Brains said. "The log was dry as a bone until I greased it."

"With what?" I snorted. "I suppose you raced all the way back to the car?"

"I reached this spot a good ten minutes before Keely did," Brains said. "I saw that he had to cross that log, so I went into the woods and got a particular species of toadstool which exudes a decidedly slippery substance when crushed. I placed a row of them along the top of the log. Then I waited."

Keely began coming to. "Look," he said. "Don't be suckers. We can split the money. If you turn me in, Ben goes too."

"I made a mistake," Ben said. "I'm going to give the money back and tell the police everything."

"You're nuts!" Keely yelped. "You want to go to the jug along with me?"

He started to put up a fight but Ben let him have a hard left on the jaw and he wilted.

A flashlight beam stabbed at us from out of the underbrush and a gruff voice said,

"Don't make a move! Raise your hands!"

In a moment, I knew the score. State Troopers had moved in.

22 THE WINDUP

THE TROOPERS HELD THE FLASHLIGHT ON US, PLAYING IT FROM one to the other.

"Two of 'em are just kids," one of the troopers said. "All right, what's been going on? Who owns that hot rod back on the road?"

Brains reached into his back pocket and pulled out his wallet. From this he took a card and handed it to one of the troopers.

"My card, sir," he said. "Slightly damp, but legible."

The tallest policeman put a light on it. He read it, then stared at Brains.

"For Pete's sake, Mike," he said. "Listen to this: 'The Benton and Carson International Detective Agency!'"

"Wha-a-t?"

"Yes, sir, we were chasing a criminal," Brains said. "We've been working on a case for weeks. This man on the ground is Joe Keely who was arrested in Middlebury yesterday. He is out on bail and was trying to leave the state."

"I own that racing car," Ben said.

177

"Kid detectives. What do you know!" a trooper said. "Sure, I know about Keely!"

"They can't prove a thing on me," Keely said when they dragged him to his feet. "Anyway, it wasn't me stole that money in Crestwood. This guy owed me plenty so I took it and—"

"What's he talking about?" a policeman asked Brains.

Ben answered for Brains. "I stole that money first," he said. "Take me to Crestwood, to the police chief there."

"Sure, we know all about that robbery, too," a trooper said. He stared closer at Brains. "Say, are you that Brains Benton they talk about?"

Brains nodded. He pointed to me. "And that's my partner, Jimmy Carson."

The trooper they called Mike shoved Joe Keely toward the woods. "All right, let's move out of here. Dan, you look after the hot rod driver. Robbery, huh? And driving a car at 140 miles per hour over a highway posted for fifty."

"It was in the interests of the law," Brains said. "We had to catch a criminal."

"Okay, Benton. We'll decide what's what later," the big trooper said.

When we got back to the road we saw two police cars there, one in front of Ben's racer, the other behind it. Three other cars were parked alongside the road. The troopers ordered the curious drivers to move on. While the trooper made some notes on a clipboard, Keely just glared at Brains and me.

They let Ben drive the racer back to Crestwood. When we got to the highway the police car carrying Joe Keely headed toward Middlebury. Brains and I rode in the police car with the trooper named Dan Riley.

"I still don't believe it," Riley said when we came in sight of Crestwood.

"I must confess it was a difficult case, Officer," Brains said.

I didn't say anything. Now that we'd solved it I wished we hadn't, in a way. It would be awful if Ben went to prison.

When we all walked into the Crestwood police station, the sergeant at the desk nearly dropped the container of coffee he had in his hand. Brains and I looked a mess all right. We were covered with dirt and grease and our clothes were soaked.

"Better get the Chief out of bed," the state trooper said.

"At this hour?" the sergeant almost yelled. "Look, he's had enough trouble with these pint-sized G-men."

Brains took the envelope from inside his shirt and put it on the sergeant's desk. "This is the money stolen from Mr. Beal's office, the Community Camp Fund money. Ben Carlin wants to make restitution."

The desk sergeant gaped at the money, then at Ben.

"That's right," Ben said. His voice shook. "I took the money."

"I've got a night's work to do yet," the state trooper said. He motioned to Ben. "Better lock him up."

"I know him pretty well," the desk sergeant said. "He won't run away."

He picked up the phone to call Chief Hadley.

Creeps, was I ever bushed. Brains kept yawning, too. The trooper said we'd better get on home, and asked if he could drop us off where we lived.

"We live only a few blocks away," Brains said. "Thanks anyway, Officer."

Dan Riley gave the desk sergeant his name and number, then took off.

"Beat it, kids," the desk sergeant said. "You can talk to the Chief in the morning."

When we left Ben said, "Thanks for what you did, you guys," and I nearly busted out crying. Thanks for what? For sending him to prison?

We flopped down on our cots in the tent a little while later and peeled off our wet clothes. If Brains said anything to me, I don't remember it. I was asleep in nothing flat.

My mother nearly fainted when I walked into the house the next morning. My clothes had dried out but they were a real mess. She let out a shriek that brought Dad out of the bathroom and down the stairs. One half of his face was still unshaved.

"Great Caesar's ghost! Where have you been? Answer me, young man!"

"You'll find out soon enough," I said. "Brains and I got back the stolen money. I can't stop to tell you now because Chief Hadley will be sending for Brains and for me any minute and I've only got time to shower and change my clothes and maybe grab some breakfast and think of what I'm going to say to—"

"Ho-old it!" Dad said. "You found the money? Where? Who stole it?"

"You've got to promise not to tell anybody until the Chief lets the news out."

"All right. All right."

"Ben Carlin," I said. "That's all I can say now."

I hurried up the stairs, leaving my mother staring after me, her mouth a big round O. Dad was hanging onto the stair banister as if he was afraid it would run away.

A police car drove up just as I was halfway through my scrambled eggs. Officer McKeon came to the door. My mother answered the bell like she was walking in her sleep.

"We came for Jimmy," the officer said. "Looks like your son is quite a hero, Mrs. Carson."

"He'll be the early death of me yet," Mom said.

Dad just sat at the table. As I left, I noticed him sprinkling sugar on his eggs. He'd already put a spoonful of salt in his coffee.

Brains was already in the police car. He seemed calm and composed and was humming *The Farmer in the Dell*.

When we walked into Chief Hadley's office, my knees turned to lumps of custard. The Mayor, the Honorable Henry J. Worthington, was there. So was Mr. Beal, and Lew Jarman. And the Chief, of course. From the way he looked at us you'd have thought Brains and I not only stole the money ourselves but had taken his watch, as well.

"Sit down!" Chief Hadley said.

We took the two empty chairs they'd saved for us. Then the Chief told Officer McKeon to bring in the prisoner.

Ben was petrified when he came in. You could tell. His eyes were red and swollen. His lips trembled.

Chief Hadley cleared his throat.

"The prisoner, Ben Carlin, has admitted everything. I took his statement last night, gentlemen. His motive was to get money enough to fix up a racing automobile and drive it in the Columbus Day race in Middlebury. He planned to pay it back with his winnings."

When the Chief paused, there was a lot of mumbling. Lew Jarman started writing in his notebook.

"Ben used his old car in the robbery. Then he pushed it into Boiling Pond. Like we all figured at the time, that store dummy was put in the car to mix up the police."

The Chief glanced toward Brains and I and scowled. Mr. Beal put his hand over his face to wipe a grin away.

Chief Hadley went through it all from start to finish. He explained that Ben had sent that letter to the police when Will Parslow had been arrested for the robbery. Ben hadn't wanted an innocent man to suffer.

The big mistake he'd made was showing up at Joe Keely's store with a big wad of money the day after the robbery. Joe put two and two together and trapped Ben into admitting he'd been the thief. Then he'd put the pressure on Ben and forced him into a partnership.

Ben told some of it himself.

"When things got hot for Keely he said we ought to throw suspicion back on Will Parslow again," Ben said. "He was sure those two young detectives, Brains and Jimmy, were finding out too much. So he had a kid drive to Crestwood and plant those checks in that nasturtium bed. I printed a note and left it where Brains and Jimmy could find it."

"Where are those checks now?" Chief Hadley snapped.

"I have them," Brains said, and took them from his coat pocket.

"You know what you've done, Benton?" the Chief yelped. "You've withheld evidence from the police! More than once, I'll wager! Now you talk, young man!"

Brother, you get to know more about Brains every day. He must have had some Daniel Webster blood in him. The only reason the Benton and Carson International Detective Agency hadn't reported certain things to Chief Hadley, Brains related, was to keep Ben Carlin's racing car a secret.

"Jimmy and I were sworn to secrecy," Brains said. "We gave Ben our solemn word."

"That's right, Chief," I said, speaking for the first time.

"Another thing," Brains said. "There were things you wouldn't have believed if we'd told you, Chief. Don't forget you ordered us to keep out of your sight."

The mayor grinned. Then Mr. Beal took the floor. He asked leniency for Ben. He said it had been pretty rough on Ben losing his parents. He'd known Ben's father and what auto racing meant to him. And it looked as if Ben was a chip off the old block.

"Anyway," Mr. Beal said, "all the money, minus three hundred dollars, has been returned. Ben has promised to make the rest good whether he wins that auto race or not. And don't forget, he risked detection sending that note in behalf of Will Parslow."

"I don't know," Chief Hadley said. "A crime has been committed here."

"The chief is right," the mayor said. "I believe Ben has learned his lesson, but the due processes of the law must be carried out. Ben must stand trial. I am sure, though, that, in view of his conduct, the decision of the court will not be too harsh."

Chief Hadley said he felt the same way.

We looked over at Ben. He grinned back at us weakly.

"Now," Mr. Beal said, "I believe it is in order to commend and congratulate these two boys, Barclay Benton and James Carson. They have endangered their lives rendering their community a great public service. They—"

The Honorable Henry J. Worthington took over again. He said all of Crestwood would be proud of us. Then he came over and shook hands with us. Everybody there did, even Chief Hadley. I don't think he wanted to, though.

We were driven home in the mayor's car with a police car leading the way, siren blaring.

My folks were on the front porch when I got out, including Dad. He'd been too excited to go down to the office. Mom kissed me. Even Ann got mushy.

People kept dropping in for the rest of the day. The phone kept ringing. Most people who called were pleased that Ben was getting a break. Not Sarah Pruett. She always wanted somebody's scalp.

My mother had a kind of relapse around the middle of the afternoon. Dad had to give her some spirits of ammonia. When she came to, she looked at me as though she hadn't seen me for a month.

"Do you realize, Jimmy Carson, you could easily have been

a very dead hero?" she said.

The next day, the *Crestwood Daily Ledger* had our pictures on the front page. The line above read: CRESTWOOD'S YOUNG HEROES OF THE HOUR.

"You might have put on something that didn't look so sloppy when you had that shot taken, Jimmy," my sister, Ann, said. "At least Brains had his hair cut."

"My darling sister," I said to Mom. "Everything is back to normal."

The only thing on my mind now was to ride downtown and get a double-sized Cherry-Fizz. I thought Brains might, for once, like one, so I dropped by the crime lab.

Brains was leaning over his desk working on a football play when I walked in.

"It's a reverse double lateral," he said. "I think I'll have it ready for Coach McIver by the time the football season opens. . . . Now you're here, Jimmy, see. And Wes Gorman gets the handoff and—"

"I'm listening," I said. I happened to notice a copy of the *Crestwood Ledger* at Brains' elbow. A small headline said:

CABIN CRUISER STOLEN AT LAKE CARMINE
Outboard Motor Taken From
Boathouse.

I sneaked the paper away and dropped it quietly into the wastebasket. I sure didn't want Brains to see that item. I felt due for a rest.

"We'll manage to get up to Lake Carmine before school opens, Operative Three," Brains said, casually without looking up. "We might just be able to catch those boat thieves."

I should have known. He didn't miss a trick.

"Oh, sure," I said. "We may still be on vacation from school, but not from the International Detective Agency."

"Correct," Brains said, looking down his long nose at me. "Crime never takes a vacation. We must always be on the job."

"I'll be ready at all times, X," I said.

What else could I say?

Whitman CLASSICS

The Hound of the
  Baskervilles

Tales to Tremble By

More Tales to Tremble By

Seven Great Detective
  Stories

Black Beauty

Tales From Arabian Nights

Little Women

The Call of the Wild

Tom Sawyer

Robin Hood

The Wonderful Wizard
  of Oz

Robinson Crusoe

Wild Animals I Have
  Known

The War of the Worlds

Stand By for Adventure

Huckleberry Finn

Alice in Wonderland

REG. U.S. PAT. OFF.

*Start your home library of
WHITMAN CLASSICS now.*

Whitman ADVENTURE and MYSTERY Books